Talon retreats [...] scowl twisting [...] to follow him. But he's my boss, and I desperately need this job. Besides, I don't think I'm ready for the kinds of games the alpha likes to play. I've heard whispers of all kinds of preferences, but Talon is a mystery and moves like a shadow through the club.

When the club opened, I put in my application immediately. Talon interviewed me in person. There were NDAs to sign. Background checks. More like an interview for employment with the FBI than to work at a club. But the job paid well, so I followed all the instructions like a good boy, ready to make a fresh start.

The black leather wristband on my left arm means I am off-limits to clients who came in but more than anything, I want Talon to ignore the rules, and take me into that private room on the second level of the club or even to a station on the main floor. I haven't seen him with anyone...yet. That doesn't mean I'll be the first. Of course, not. But I want to be the last.

Such a Good Omega is the first book in His Alpha Desires, the highly anticipated M/M Mpreg shifter series by USA Today Bestselling Author Lorelei M. Hart and featuring the members and staff of the hottest new club in town. Such a Good Omega features an alpha club owner who seems aloof, an omega who can't stop fantasizing about his boss, sweet heat, sizzling heat, new beginnings, healing, true love, fated mates, an adorable baby (or two), and a guaranteed HEA.

The unauthorized reproduction or distribution of a copyrighted work is illegal. Criminal copyright infringement, including infringement without monetary gain, is investigated by the FBI and is punishable by fines and federal imprisonment.

Please purchase only authorized electronic editions and do not participate in, or encourage, the electronic piracy of copyrighted materials. Your support of the author's rights is appreciated.

This book is a work of fiction. Names, characters, places, and incidents are the products of the author's imagination or used fictitiously. Any resemblance to actual events, locales or persons, living or dead, is entirely coincidental.

Such a Good Omega
Copyright © 2024 by Lorelei M. Hart
Digital ISBN 979-8-89320-083-6
Print ISBN 979-8-89320-084-3

All rights reserved. Except for use in any review, the reproduction or utilization of this work, in whole or in part, in any form by any electronic, mechanical or other means now known or hereafter invented, is forbidden without the written permission of the publisher.

Such a Good Omega

By

Lorelei M. Hart

Chapter One

Rowan

"Rowan James." A man wearing a black button-down shirt paired with black slacks called my name. His hair was slicked back and his skin flawless. Almost not human, almost looking so perfect he was robotic.

He worked here already. If he was the kind of person the owners of Cuffed were looking for, then I'd lost the job before the interview even started.

"Right here," I said, standing.

"Follow me, Mr. James." His voice was iced velvet gliding over my skin. All the interviewees had been seated in a room with black walls with black leather chairs, simple. Plain. Minimalist. No paintings on the walls or fake flowers that hadn't been dusted like other places I'd been.

The man glided in front of me while I gawked at the place I hoped to work. Everything was black. Even the knobs and hinges on the many doors.

Unlike the waiting room, the hallway walls had pictures of erotic and yet tasteful images. A hint of vanilla and sandalwood flowed from an air-conditioning vent.

Everything about this place oozed sex.

Hell. I already wanted to be a member, and I'd never been into anything kink.

"Mr. Marwood's office is here. Please wait while I make sure he is ready for you."

Mr. Marwood? As in Talon Marwood, the co-owner of the club? Shit. I thought I would be interviewing with an assistant or a human resources manager.

Certainly not one of the owners.

Mr. Robotic and Perfect came out of the office in seconds and bowed at the waist the slightest bit. "Mr. Marwood is waiting your arrival."

My feet wouldn't move. My breathing stopped, and the only thing I could hear was the booming drum of my heart pounding between my ears, threatening to blow my temples.

"I-I..." I looked for some excuse as to why I was mimicking a statue.

"Let's be prompt and not keep Mr. Marwood waiting, Rowan. One foot in front of the other. We're not open yet, so no one here is going to bite." He winked, practically shoved me into the office, and shut the door behind me.

The walls were black leather panels. The floors ebony-colored wood with both matte and shiny designs in the grain. In front of me was a massive desk and leather executive chair with its back turned to me, also in the same color as all the rest.

"Take a seat, Mr. James. There's no reason to be nervous."

Could he tell? Had the other guy told him something? He couldn't even see me.

I sat in one of two of the leather guest chairs in front of his bus of a desk and smoothed my shirt with sweaty hands.

"I can hear your heartbeat, in case you were wondering."

I nodded but then muttered something close to okay.

Everything depended on finding a job, and this one paid the most. I needed this.

The tall chair turned and my life spun on its axis. I'd seen some pictures online, but only silhouettes and his back. In person, Talon Marwood was hands down the most beautiful man I'd ever seen. His dark-brown hair was cut close on the sides, left longer on top. His chiseled jawline immediately had me wondering how good it would feel to kiss my way down its path, making him moan.

His green eyes made me ache in places that I'd thought dormant after everything I'd been through.

"Rowan James," he said, clearing his throat. "Your resume is impeccable. Everyone on your reference list spoke highly of you. Your last boss said he had to hire three other people to fill your shoes."

Heat crawled up the back of my neck and settled in my cheeks. "Travis was a tough but fair manager. I'm glad he was pleased with my work."

A flash of gold took over Talon's eyes as he cocked his head. "You find yourself eager to please your boss?"

He was talking about the job, but I read way more into that question.

"Of course. Following the rules and going above expectations makes me proud of a job well done."

Talon grunted. He was dressed similar to the man who had led me here but with much more style and grace, which I found hard to believe since the other man was so put together. His crisp black button-down shirt rolled to the elbows revealed designs that spread up his forearms. "I see. We've looked over everything, but I do have one last question." I saw something metal in his mouth. Oh. Oh my. Talon's tongue was pierced.

Gods, my wolf was panting at the alpha across the desk from me.

"Please," I responded.

He growled deep inside his chest. The sound was low, barely there, but I heard it and to my wolf, it was a howl for me.

"Your previous employer did mention you left without giving proper notice."

The question I didn't want to answer. But for the man across for me, I would spill just about any secret. Didn't know why. He was a brooding shadow that I was sure not very many could capture, but I trusted him. So did my animal.

"I needed to leave town as soon as possible. To get away from an abusive partner. I didn't have a choice. I apologized to Travis. I had no choice," I repeated, knowing full well the answer to the question might stain any of my work history or praise from former bosses and references.

His once-green eyes clouded with a storm I couldn't decipher. Was he that angry that I had left without notice? Had I tanked this interview before I had a chance?

"Rowan, I've seen everything I need to see."

My heart dipped. I was hoping for this position but even more than that, if I didn't get hired, I would probably never see Talon again, and somehow the thought had me on the verge of tears.

"I understand." I stood, but he held up his hand.

"Not so fast. If you allow me to finish. Please. Sit back down."

I plopped into the seat. "I apologize."

"No need. Rowan, I'd like to hire you for a bartender position. Really I'd like to have you as one of the bar managers but we've already filled those positions."

Tingling sensations wrapped around me. "Really?"

Talon chuckled, and I had a feeling that was a rare sound. "Really. You're well qualified, and we would love to have you on the team. Let's go over some things and then I'll send you over to HR so you can fill out the mountains of paperwork and we can pay you. Plus, we offer full benefits for all employees."

I must've thanked him three million times before he was able to go on with his rules.

"The dress code is all black like Samuel is wearing. The person who walked you in. And here."

He pulled a thick leather cuff from his desk drawer. It was stamped with the logo of the club and I reached for it, but he pulled back. "Allow me."

He leaned on the edge of his desk and motioned for my arm. Certainly he didn't do this with all his new employees. Or perhaps he did and there was no reason for my cock to twitch and my heart rate to soar with anticipation.

I raised my arm, but he shook his head. "Left one." I raised the other, obediently. He gently put the cuff on my wrist, staring into my eyes all the while, and snapped it into place. I moved to put my arm down, but he covered the cuff with his large, warm hand. His fingers rested on the inside of my arm, and everything in me lit up instantly.

"Keep this on at all times in this club. It marks you as an employee and will save you from unwanted groping and being accidentally pulled into things you don't want to be pulled into. A gorgeous omega like you needs to keep this on at all times. Now, I insist on giving you a tour before you go to HR."

"Are you sure?" I asked. "Someone else can do that."

"I'm giving you the tour, Rowan."

"Yes, Sir." The words flowed from my mouth. I was always respectful as possible and had always called bosses sir, but the words meant something else here.

One of Talon's eyebrows raised. "Sir is not my preference, though it sounds so alluring from your lips."

I ducked my head a bit. "I'm sorry. Yes, Talon."

He growled again, bass and slow. "Let's go before I change my mind."

He guided me through the club. I had to admit, all of this was intimidating as hell. I'd never been into a sex club before, but the idea of coming here and having the freedom to express my sexual and intimate needs safely sounded like something I might want to explore. Not with strangers, of course, but with someone I trusted.

I had a full, fiery blush through the whole thing. Ropes. Straps. Handcuffs. Whips. Contraptions that gave me more questions than answers. Leather. So much leather.

"That's all of it," Talon said. "Do you have any questions?"

"Um, actually I do. Do employees have member access on their days off?"

Those clouds rolled into his eyes again as he flicked out his tongue and licked his lips. "You make me want to ask about all your preferences, Rowan. All your deep desires." He sighed. "HR is right through that door. I look forward to seeing you around."

I felt dismissed. Hollow even. I turned to watch him leave, needing a little more torture, but he slipped through a panel and it silently closed behind him. I went through the door and sat at the desk that I was waved toward.

"Welcome to the club." The man typed all kinds of information into the computer and asked for my ID and Social Security card. "You must be something special."

"Why do you say that?" I asked.

"Because that interview with Talon was the longest I've ever seen him grant. Usually, he's a five-minute interviewer. Goes with his gut. And he's never given a tour to anyone. I mean anyone."

Chapter Two

Talon

I canceled the rest of the interviews, having completed our initial hiring with Rowan. He was well qualified as either a bartender or bar manager, based on his resume and his former employer's comments, but nothing reflected any experience at a venue like ours. But some of his comments definitely indicated a healthy curiosity. One very tempting to satisfy.

When I left him with HR, I found myself wanting to go back and make sure it was going okay, see if he had any more questions, be sure he didn't change his mind about wanting to work at Cuffed. If that did happen, I'd be in the unenviable position of not being able to contact him because using information provided for consideration for employment was not for personal use.

During the tour, I kept catching myself looking over at him, gauging his reactions. Bartenders were known for keeping their cool, and Rowan was no different, but they were also notoriously good at hiding their reactions. With everyone and their dysfunctional brother dumping their personal problems on the guy mixing their martini, it took a certain personality not to absorb all the angst. Finally realizing how ridiculous it was for me to hang around outside HR, I dragged myself away. There was plenty for me to do as we got close to opening. Our contractor was the best, but I wanted flawless—not something probably humanly possible.

Every detail had been gone over multiple times. Unlike common opinion, black was not black. There were so many tones and hues and shades, and our goal had been to use them to create a unique design, a goal I believed we'd reached with success. I paced through the main dungeon area, where the stations were installed and ready to go.

The spider, spanking benches, cages, and other dungeon furnishings stood apart from one another with plenty of walking space in between and as much room as any activity required. Whips, for example, not only needed a large space to avoid hitting passersby but so that the wielder could avoid harming their play partner because they couldn't use their arm properly. Overhead lights illuminated each station with lots of settings the lighting director could control from his space near the DJ booth. A stage for live music and small dance floor stood at the other end of the room from the dungeon area.

It was a huge room, and when we'd been planning the build, I'd wondered if we could even fill all that space, but now that everything was installed, I almost wished we had a few hundred more square feet.

The main floor's high ceiling allowed for balcony seating and observing everything at the stations below. Charcoal-gray leather banquette seating lined the walls, and tables scattered about the floor, within viewing range of all the action but not within the actual "play area."

I moved from station to station, as I had done every day since they were in place, but this time something was different. At each, I imagined a certain omega submitting to my ministrations. Bound to the spanking bench with his round butt cheeks exposed for a lusty spanking. For example. One of my favorite stations was fire play, and a dom had to have a great deal of experience to use that in our club. Everything could be dangerous, but fire required care and technique. A skill I'd acquired a decade before and enjoyed.

"Hey, Talon?" One of my partners in this enterprise dropped a hand on my shoulder. "Hello?"

I jumped then laughed. "Alex, you startled me. Is something wrong?"

"No, just wondering how long you're going to stare at the fire play table with that bemused expression. Can we count on a demonstration of your talent soon?"

"I imagine. Not right away but eventually." Maybe if a certain omega would like to try it out. He'd been so shy, but everything about him drew me. "How are things in the kitchens? All the supplies come in?"

"Most." He ran a finger over the smooth leather of a spanking bench. "Soft on the submissive's skin."

"Yes. But what do you mean 'most'?"

"Oh, one box went missing." He snorted. "And of course it was high-end seafood for the special opening-night apps."

"And?"

"And they are replacing it. Immediately. They weren't all that helpful at first, but when I offered to return everything they did deliver, they saw the light."

"Very good." Alex was dominant in all things, even if the supplier might not realize the tools he employed to achieve his aims. "And the staff?"

"Filled the last bartender position today. The guy is in with HR dealing with the paperwork, and there we go!"

Such a Good Omega

We walked the floor together, talking about all the details one more time. We'd been working on this project for years, if you included the original planning stages, and it was hard to believe we were finally about to open the doors. Membership applications had been coming in for a while, and the staff member in charge of that had been full-time and then some. We were charging a steep membership fee, but just having the money did not get anyone through the doors. Research into their past, references, previous club associations... If they passed all of that, there was an interview with two of the owners to get past.

Time consuming, sure, but we believed it worth the effort.

Alex left me to return to the kitchen and see if the seafood had arrived. He wanted to be sure that the quality matched the price. We were all detail-oriented, no matter what other skills we had. It was why we were a good team, and I hoped would have the club we'd dreamed of. Doms, sure. But also dreamers.

Chapter Three

Rowan

There's always a time in between jobs where you get a new position but you don't have enough money to buy the things you need for the next job—because you've been unemployed.

It was precarious to say the least.

"What are you up to today?" Artemis asked, knocking on the frame of my open bedroom door.

"I think I'm going to try and apply for some credit to buy the new clothes for my job."

"So, you got it?" He beamed and stepped inside the room and sat on my bed. Artemis was a good roommate. We split everything evenly and cooked for each other. Never fussed over who was going to clean what and when. We were both hardworking and kept tidy.

"I did. I'm nervous and excited at the same time."

"What's the deal with the new cuff?" he asked.

"Oh." I stared at it. Seemed a shame to take it off when Talon had put it on me with such care. It was a piece of him, to me. "It's for the club. They gave it to me. It tells the members that I work there and am off-limits."

"Damn. I mean, what if you're not on shift and don't want to be off-limits."

I whirled in my chair. Artemis was already dressed for the day despite having the day off from work. "I kind of asked the same question."

"And?" he asked.

"And nothing."

I had thought about Talon almost nonstop since leaving the club. The way he looked at me. Growled, not in an aggressive way but as a possessive alpha. He touched me with such tenderness. Always made eye contact.

A great urge to please him had taken root deep in my soul. To hear his preferences. To make them manifest and hear the words of praise pour from his lips.

And even, to my surprise, to let him punish me if I did something wrong.

But at the end of every fantasy, reality slapped me in the face with its icy hand. An alpha like that? Put together. Clearly successful, with the most attractive omegas at his feet? Why in the world would he look twice at an omega like me?

I'd convinced myself that my interview was nothing more than him taking pity on me.

And it would take a lot to change my mind.

"I've got an idea," Arty blurted. "How about I take you shopping?"

I laughed. "The shopping isn't the problem. I have no money. Hence, the applying for credit."

"Yeah, but anything you order, you're not going to get in on time. Let me treat you for once. I have a ton of money in savings. I can spare some for a friend. You can even pay me back if you like. Let me help. You have been moping around here for a while. I've seen you try and try to get a job. You look so damned happy. Please."

I blew out a long breath. It felt like stealing from him. Taking something that wasn't mine. I earned my own way in this world and I prided myself on it.

"Rowan, you'd do it for me if the roles were swapped, right?"

He nailed me with that one. "Yes."

"Then let me do this for you. I'm offering. You didn't ask. At least two outfits so you can switch out and wash them. You need to look sharp for Cuffed. That place is swanky."

Swanky. Not the word I would use, but he was right. I couldn't show up in one of those button-downs from the discount store. The ones that came with a clip-on tie included.

"I do have to look nice to get bigger tips."

Artemis clapped. "Now we're talking. Get your shoes on. Let's go."

We went to a place I'd never heard of in a strip mall about an hour from our apartment. Artemis said he knew the owner and that he would give us some good prices. We arrived at a fancy shop that sold tuxes and suits.

"This is too expensive," I said as Arty put the car into park.

"Trust me, okay? Kenny knows what he's doing."

Once inside, Kenny said he had some suits and other things in the back we might be interested in. Apparently, pretty often, people ordered suits and outfits and paid but never picked them up. He came out with shirts and pants, all in black, of course, and deeply discounted because they had been left.

Kenny was a master, that much I knew. I'd never worn things that fit me the way Kenny dressed me. Each one tailored as though made for me.

By the time we were done, I had five pairs of pants and shirts plus two belts fit for kings but at discount store prices. Artemis insisted I get a pair of nice shoes along with socks because no one wanted to see a man with white socks when his black clothes were impeccable.

He wasn't wrong.

I hung up everything in my closet after telling Arty about a hundred times how grateful I was.

Tomorrow was my first day and while I was excited to work again and feel like I was contributing to my life in a financial way, I craved seeing Talon.

Except he was my boss and I shouldn't feel that way.

Clearly, that didn't stop me.

That night, I tossed and turned until I couldn't stand my bed anymore. I got up and went to my computer and fed my new hunger.

I searched for Talon Marwood in the search engine, feeling like a fool for wanting to stare at his images, even if they were nothing more than the back of his head or a blurry silhouette.

Except this time when I searched, there were no results. None. It was as though they had been wiped from the internet.

Such a Good Omega

Damn it.

Good thing I would get to see him tomorrow night.

Chapter Four

Talon

Our grand opening was no more public knowledge than the small, subtle sign by the door done up in neon lights. Everything about a club like Cuffed was private. Not only the members went through background checks, but every staff member down to the busboys and the janitorial staff had to be cleared and agree to keep the members' business private. When the mayor and half the city council arrived for the first night, they were accompanied by a politician of much greater standing.

These people did not want the voters to know what their preferences were in their private lives. And while I would find it tiresome to have to pretend to be someone other than I was, I understood that some people's choices of career put them in the sights of those who would judge them for their lifestyle.

So, while nobody cut a ribbon in front of the building, we celebrated our first night in our own way. A live band played on the stage, we had a buffet of all kinds of appetizers and mini desserts, and drinks were discounted for those who did not require top shelf.

We did not have the stations open for play, but we did have demonstrations by some of the staff and their submissives for those who might not know exactly what to do with a given piece of equipment. I walked around, as did my business partners, greeting people and discussing the club's hours and policies and showing off some of the private themed rooms as well. We did not have all of them fitted out yet because craftsmen were still working on some elements, but enough to create a real buzz among the membership.

We had a limited staff this evening, since only platinum members were invited, so we chose the employees who'd been hired on earlier and were already trained, but I missed seeing the omega bartender and looked forward to his first day.

Pausing by a spanking bench, I watched the dom guide his submissive into position, the angle set so his buttocks lifted high and proud. A group of members already circled the station, sharing their thoughts on the scene. The dom flicked a glance at them, and they hushed, their silence pregnant with anticipation. This particular dominant was in high demand with single submissives at the club he'd worked at before, and I felt confident the watchers knew this.

Edward rubbed the sub's thighs, eliciting a groan before turning his attention to his bottom. "Are you in a hurry, subbie? Do you crave pain so much?"

"No."

"Is that honest?" He drew back his palm and smacked across both cheeks, the crack drawing a soft inhale from the watchers. "And is that how you address me?"

"No, Sir. It was not honest. I do crave pain...but I was embarrassed."

Edward bent and whispered something in his ear, and the sub shuddered from head to toe. "I have a long line of bottoms to spank tonight. So no more lies."

"Only the truth, Sir. Please. Hard."

"Are you saying you're hard? You're not going to get our new spanking bench all sticky, are you?"

"I'll try not to...oof!" The next slap landed on his left cheek, the third on the right, then next on the very sensitive sit spot. Edward wasn't teasing anymore, and his openhanded spanks had the sub writhing on the slippery bench.

"Do I need to strap you down?"

"Yes, Sir." His breathing was harsh fluttery. "I can't stay still."

The bench was well equipped for this contingency, and Edward fastened belts around his waist and spread thighs. We did have policies for cleaning the equipment between uses, the work done by the players, and if the dom kept going the way he began, it would be a real mess. The sub's trembling had increased, his panting loud enough for those of us who stood nearby to hear. Which was why the dom stopped and just stroked his reddened skin for a few minutes.

Edward held the whole crowd in his thrall, and when he reached for the crop dangling from his belt, everything amped up to another level. Running it up the man's leg, he whispered something to him again and the sub nodded. The crop painted a line of welts across the red skin.

I leaned in closer too, always fascinated by someone who knew what they were doing. After tonight, most of the stations would be occupied by members, but demos would continue from time to time, just as part of the experience. Spanking was one of the most basic things that would go on here, but it was always popular both for those involved and an audience. There were a lot of ways to do it, but Edward was a master. He enjoyed other activities as well, and he was not really serious about the long line for tonight. He was all about quality and not quantity, and he'd torment this one sub for as long as the man was up for it. Then he'd provide aftercare.

If he truly was the pain slut he claimed, that could be all evening.

And I had other things to do, so I left the station and its interested watchers and continued on to meet other guests and make sure everything was running smoothly. So far, I'd call it an excellent opening night. Tomorrow, we'd be open to all members, and I anticipated a busy night.

I didn't get home until very late, so I allowed myself a little extra sleep in the morning, but my workday began long before the doors opened and so by ten o'clock, I was at my desk and reviewing the reports from the night before. We hadn't expected to make a profit since we had the buffet and other freebies for the guests, but to my pleasure we didn't lose any money at least.

And I had some instructions for the bartenders and servers, and a camera on the bar area when Samuel passed the instructions along. They weren't

Such a Good Omega

allowed into my office and were all sworn to never go in there, or get fired. I watched Rowan while this was explained, and his expression told the story. Yeah, the omega is interested, but I will never fully trust an omega again.

Chapter Five

Rowan

The great thing about Cuffed, other than being the place I was almost guaranteed to make huge tips and actually be able to pay my rent without scrimping, was that it was within walking distance of my apartment.

I made sure to get to the club a half hour before my official start time because one of my dads had drilled into me from a young age that on time was late and early was on time. We were that family who arrived fifteen minutes before an event and read a book until it was time to go in.

"Good evening, Rowan," Samuel greeted me at the employee door. "You showed up early. Good man. Let's move to the table over here. I have everything you need."

There was a bit more pep in my step tonight as I followed him.

It was definitely the clothes. Artemis said I looked like a million dollars and whistled as I turned around. He said if he wasn't only into dominant alphas, he might make a move on his roommate.

I took it as a compliment.

"Sorry we didn't have this ready when you were hired. There was a hangup with the tech. Here is your badge. Please wear it around your neck at all times. It will get you into the computers at the bar as well as clocking in and out and access to the employee entrance. Oh, and the employee break room and bathroom. Looks like we aren't missing anything in your files. You've been given the tour, I heard?"

I nodded. Blushing already. Talon had an effect on me that never faded.

"Good. Everyone else isn't as prompt as you, but I'm starting the daily lineup in five. Any questions or concerns before we start? About anything you heard or experienced last night in the training?"

"No. I have this, and I know how to pour drinks. I should be fine."

I had been emailed the menu the night before and had memorized it to the best of my ability but was also told there would be a cheat sheet at the bar, especially since it was the first day for us and the club.

After Samuel gave his briefing, we learned that three employees had quit and so, while they expected a hectic night, it would be even more because of the shortage.

I couldn't take my mind off of Talon. Waiting for him to walk in. Maybe order a drink from me. I wondered what his favorite drink would be. What he did while he was in that back office, the one we were forbidden to enter.

Gods, why was it that the words "forbidden" and "Talon" together made me even more hungry to know him?

Insane didn't even explain how my shift was going. I kept my eyes mostly on my work but couldn't help but notice the things happening around me.

I'd had to sidestep grabs and pinches despite the leather cuff, while trying to help some waiters catch up on their deliveries. After that, I stayed behind the bar. Some people came in with rings on their right hand, differing fingers. I'd learned from a fellow bartender that the rings meant different preferences. All silicone rings. Red. Gold. Silver. White. One that was turquoise. It meant the person was open to anything and everything. They'd gone over some of the ring meanings the night before, but the teal-colored one hadn't been mentioned.

I found it all fascinating. People came here because it was safe. Because they could express their interests without judgment or the sneers and rejections of others.

Talon and his partners had created a bubble of freedom.

My phone buzzed. Unlike other jobs, we were encouraged to check texts for updates and important messages about work. I checked the message from an unknown number.

Bring a Dark and Stormy to Talon's office. His personal request. Delivered by you.

Immediately I scoffed. Sure, the message outlined one of my fantasies about bringing Talon a drink to his office and him drinking me up instead, but I wasn't falling for this bullshit. This was a test. It had to be a test.

And I needed this job too much to be that gullible.

I stuffed my phone back in my pocket and got back to work. The tips were piling in and the computer system kept track of the servers and how much tips they were earning like a competition board. Samuel said it encouraged all of us to be better to earn more money. I supposed a little healthy competition never hurt anyone and he was right. We all checked the numbers...a lot.

I leaned back against the counter and took a breath and down an iced coffee. Servers could have anything nonalcoholic on shift.

"You're doing well," Samuel said, sidling up to me.

"I'm trying." I shrugged.

"You really are doing well. In fact, I have a note from one of the owners. He called me in and gave me this himself."

I took the folded piece of paper and opened it. The words shocked me.

Bring me a drink. Your choice. I want it delivered personally, Rowan.

Talon.

"This has to be a joke. I'm not falling for this. We're not supposed to go into Talon's office. At all."

Samuel nodded and moved a bit closer than he had been before. "Trust me, Rowan. It's okay. We don't really say no to one of the owners but especially Talon. He never requests anything like this."

"Okay," I relented. If they tried to fire me, I had this note as proof, and Samuel would back me up.

I hoped. I made the Dark and Stormy that so well fit Talon and walked toward his office.

My stomach balled up in knots as I raised my hand to knock on the door.

"Enter," he barked, and instantly my channel became slick as though he were talking to that part of me specifically.

I walked in slowly, waiting for the reprimand. I knew better. Damn it. I knew better.

"It's okay, Rowan. I gave permission for you to bring me a drink. It wasn't a test. You're not in trouble."

I stayed put, feet frozen in place.

"Rowan, look at me." I did. Gods, he knew how to command me. "Bring me my drink."

Shaking my head, I rounded his ginormous desk and offered the drink to him. He lifted the glass to his lips and took a sip. "This is delicious, Rowan. Just perfect. You did an excellent job. Not only with the drink but at following the rules." His eyes roamed me, and I shivered. "So, so good."

I swallowed, absorbing every breath of praise from him. His words and worship struck me in the chest and filled me with heat. Tears began to well in my eyes but I demanded they retreat. I would not cry in front of this strong alpha.

Chapter Six

Talon

This submissive omega blossomed at praise. If I said the least nice thing about how he made a drink or anything at all, his cheeks flamed, and a little smile lifted the corners of his mouth. I'd met a few like him, but none who caught my attention every time he walked by like Rowan did.

I'd never gone out with an employee, although club life could sometimes blur the edges of relationships. We did not have a rule against anyone dating as long as everyone was in full consent. Just like anything that happened at Cuffed.

Staff did not get a free membership, but members did have passes that could be used, as long as their guest submitted info for a background check. Since Rowan had already been through that for his job, it could be skipped in his case.

When he brought my drink in, I knew I needed to exercise care and make sure that what I wanted to ask him did not read in a way that made him feel compelled. Oh, I would enjoy giving him orders, but only once we'd reached complete agreement on how that would look. And he'd have to be comfortable with having two completely separate roles together.

There was no guarantee we'd work out. I certainly didn't have a good experience last time, and I'd planned to stay single for a good long time. Preferably forever. Opening the club seemed like the best way to do that, to have plenty of omega subs to scene with, no ties that bind.

I didn't believe in fated mates. Not anymore.

And as he stood there in front of me, I studied him carefully. I'd noticed how he responded to any positive words at his interview. "This is delicious, Rowan. Just perfect. You did an excellent job. Not only with the drink but at following the rules." His tongue darted out to wet his lips, and he shivered. "So, so good."

I went rock-hard.

"Thank you, Sir." Did he even know what it meant when he said that? He was not in the lifestyle yet. But he had expressed interest.

"How is your night going so far? Everyone being helpful?"

"Absolutely. I think it's making it easier that we're all new. I know some of the others were hired earlier and had more training, but as to real customers, we're all pretty much on a level field."

"And you have experience," I reminded him. "Bartending is bartending, wouldn't you say?"

"In many ways, yes. There are special drinks here, of course, but the biggest difference from most bars is how people behave."

"Yes?" I waited for him to say he had a problem with all the kink. Or that it made him uncomfortable.

"Very respectful. Courteous even. It's nice for a change."

"Was your last bar a rough place?" I didn't like the thought of him having to deal with ruffians.

"No, I think it was typical actually. I've never been in a club like this before, not even for a visit and I don't know what I expected, but it's a pleasant surprise." He hesitated. "It's only my first night though. Maybe it's not always like this?"

"It will be." Even if it wasn't always the way we intended it to be, it would be for him. "I'm glad you're happy here, on your first day."

I had him sit down, and we spoke a little more. He had some very good observations about his fellow employees and how the manager had things set up. Once again, I regretted that I hadn't had that position open for him because he had a keen mind for organization.

Finally, after ten minutes or so, it was time to send him back to the bar. His manager wouldn't appreciate him disappearing even to speak with one of the bosses. "When is your next night off, Rowan?"

"I have no idea. I just started. Why?"

"Give me a moment." I logged in to the schedule. "You're off in three days."

"Oh, okay. Thank you." His brows drew together in puzzlement, and I wanted to reach out a finger and smooth them. "Did you want me to take off so soon?"

"No, I didn't set the schedule. I just wondered when there might be a night that you could come to the club as my guest. If you'd like to."

"I don't...I mean yes. Of course, but I've never done anything that happens here. Is it all right?"

"Come and hang out with me and we can play it by ear." I came around the desk and sat on the edge. "I promise nobody will flog you without your consent."

"Flogging? Is that what you like to do?"

I shrugged. "Sometimes. Is that something you might like to try?"

His eyes were so wide I could see the white almost all the way around; his voice so low I had to lean closer to hear. "Maybe."

Oh, omega.

I brushed a kiss over his parted lips then moved back around my desk. "Then, be my guest and we'll observe. See what you are interested in. Then we can negotiate."

Chapter Seven

Rowan

When I'd been asked out before, there had been no contact in between. Someone asked me out and days later, they would pick me up and we would get to know each other.

But with Talon, everything since I brought him that first drink felt like foreplay.

The way he talked to me. The way he complimented me when I did something well, which was often, apparently. His words were more than empty phrases. I felt adored when he spoke to me, as though they were coming from his heart.

His end-of-the-shift kisses had become more and more demanding and possessive. Our hands roamed over one another in hungry, greedy motions.

I'd never been so ready for an alpha to this degree. I was sure I could explode with an orgasm the minute he got inside me. Hell, maybe before that.

When my ex, Salem, asked me out for the first time, it was more of a demand. I went along, as the people-pleaser I was. I felt privileged that a man, an alpha, strong and beautiful like him would ever stoop to go out with someone like me.

Boy, he must've seen me coming from a mile away.

The abuse started on our second date. Of course, I made excuses for it in the beginning. Things that were blaring, on fire, red flags, I chalked up as possessive or taking charge like a good alpha should. Except, I always thought those things should have some care and concern about them.

I had been wrong.

Salem wanted to control every facet of my life and when I disagreed or held my ground, there was hell to be paid. At first, it was the silent treatment or withholding affection or sex. The first time he slapped me, I cried and apologized. I remember that moment, crouching in the corner, crying, sobbing, wondering what I could've done better or how I would try harder.

I didn't even know who I was anymore.

He'd made me question myself and who I was.

"That's a pretty big damned frown for someone going on a hot date with a millionaire," Artemis said.

I shook my head of the treacherous memories. "I should be, but for the life of me I can't figure out to wear." My roommate didn't need to know that my ex was in my head, even now, when I and my wolf were sure we'd found our fated mate in the body of a god and the boss of the best job I'd ever had.

"You're going to the club, right?" Artemis asked. He came and began to rifle through my closet.

"Yes. But as a guest."

He did a dance at that. "So, we don't want to wear all black because that's what he sees you in all the...oh my god, I have the perfect outfit." He bolted from the room at a sprint and came back with a garment bag. "I have these pants that I bought on deep discount. They are a little snug on me but I know they will fit you. It's really a suit, but you won't need the jacket. There's a vest and...trust me?"

I shrugged. "Sure. Why not."

"That's not reassuring but I will prove you wrong."

Less than a half hour later, Artemis had me looking like I'd walked right out of a fashion TikTok post.

Hashtag Hot Omega.

"Color me impressed," I said, admiring myself in the mirror. He'd paired the dark-navy-blue pants and vest with a pale-pink button-up shirt, rolled at the sleeve.

"You won't need this," he said, and pointed to my cuff. Gods, I hadn't taken it off since Talon put it on me and didn't want to now.

But tonight, I was no employee. I was Talon Marwood's date.

I'd been reading up on the lifestyle. I wanted as much information as possible and I had to admit, some of what I read was scary.

Scary with a stranger. Scary with someone I didn't trust completely.

I knew that Talon would never hurt me. Maybe it was shifter instinct or a hunch, but I did trust him.

"Did I tell you that he said I was the only one who could deliver him drinks?" I asked, looking for a pair of shoes that would fit my outfit.

"You did."

I laughed. "And how much he compliments me? He told me there has never been a more gorgeous omega in the world."

"You told me that too," Artemis laughed. "And the dark-brown pair. Don't ruin my outfit."

I grabbed for the shoes and put on the navy-blue socks Artemis picked out to match. I'd showered and used my expensive cologne, the one that I saved for special occasions.

Artemis cleared his throat. "None of my business but...have you chosen a safe word?"

"Is it stupid that I want something weird but also, I don't want him to laugh at me for my choice?"

Artemis pursed his lips. "Does he seem like the type to laugh at you, Rowan? From what I've heard, he's all about building you up, not tearing you down."

I blew out a breath. "I think I know what I'll use but I'm not telling you. I have to keep some things secret."

"Okay," Artemis said and got up to leave. "But I need details on the sexy time, and you know as well as I do that there will be sexy time. I mean, it's a date at a sex club."

"Maybe." I shrugged.

There was a chance that Talon only wanted to play. I knew from the other bartenders that all play didn't lead to sex.

Still, I thought I would explode the first time he touched my naked skin.

Gods, I hoped Talon wanted to do more than play.

Chapter Eight

Talon

A half hour before Rowan was expected to arrive, I left my office and went to the foyer. People stopped at a desk there to leave their phones to be locked away. It was one of our most important rules related to privacy of our guests. They could also leave them in their car if they preferred, but they were not getting them past the front desk. Even with all the background checks, I'd heard of other clubs where journalists or influencers managed to convince a member to take pictures and pass them along. Once that happened, the owners of a club were regarded as no longer trustworthy. With good reason.

The desk attendant would also direct those who reserved them to changing rooms or private rooms and provided other services. We were busy, and she had no time to chat me up, although the arriving members did. I wasn't always present, with so much work to do in my office, and I had yet to demo fire or anything else. They were mostly either saying how much they liked the club or asking me when I was going to demo, and I thanked them for their kind comments and told them soon. Keeping it vague.

Rowan showed up early, as I'd expected, and I showed him how to check in as a guest before leading him into the main club area. "It feels so strange to be here and not be working."

I reached for his hand and pulled him close into my side. "We won't be playing tonight, so why don't we get a drink and walk around. You can see the various stations and what goes on there. Things you can't do while trapped behind a bar."

"Okay. I think I'd like a drink."

I skipped the line and walked right up to the bar, the crowd parting in front of me. There had to be some advantage to being an owner. Then I guided him from station to station, watching his reactions as much as explaining what was going on. He didn't seem to like a lot of the impact play, except for spanking, but he liked the electrical and when we got to the fire bench, where a steamer trunk stood as well, filled with items that would be needed for safe play, he stopped.

"How come nobody is here?" It was the only unoccupied station. "And what is in the chest?"

"Good question. Want to see and take a guess on what type of kink goes on here?" I winked at him. "Want a hint?"

"Sure!"

"It's my special skill."

He squeezed my arm. "Now I really want to know." Dropping to his knees, he lifted the lid of the restored antique that had made its way across the Atlantic on an ocean liner over a century before. It had stickers inside, faded and glossed over with a coat of lacquer to preserve them. A steel bowl, a bottle of alcohol, a second bowl with a folded cloth in it, and other items, including a fire extinguisher and first aid supplies. Others who used the station did not have access to my personal belongings, but would need to bring their own. I had carried my tools in a leather satchel before I had this chest.

"Fire play. It's not usually out here because I prefer to keep my things in my private playroom, but I am going to be doing a demo later in the week, so it's out here for the time being."

"You have a private playroom?" Interesting that his question wasn't *What is fire play?* He hadn't seen it here, since my demo would be the first time on the floor. "Can we go there? Is there a bed?"

Not a spanking bench... He was curious, but reserved. "Would you prefer privacy when you are with your dom?" I teased. "Should I take you there now?"

"I would like to know more," he said, not meeting my eyes. "Sir."

"Let's go now, then, before we end up in conversation with someone and can never get away." I had no trouble making people look away, but going to my playroom with Rowan sounded way better than sharing him with the general population.

We barely made it into the playroom before I had him in my arms. I'd imagined we'd experiment with kink before vanilla lovemaking, but this omega knew what he wanted. And, for once, I had no objection to stripping his clothes off and getting a look at what lay beneath. This omega was perfection, lean muscle and lightly furred chest that would have to be shaved if he wanted to do fire play on his front side.

I didn't have a large bed, but a daybed where I could nap if I chose or even spend the night if I worked late. It was not luxurious but comfortable, and as I pressed him into the mattress, he looked up at me with glowing eyes. "You going to undress anytime soon, alpha?"

"I thought you might like a head start." I dragged him to the edge of the bed and knelt between his spread legs.

"Bad pun."

"But good head." I closed my mouth around him, licking and sucking and going much faster than I normally would. I loved making an omega wait for it, but this one was different. In ways I couldn't begin to imagine. I'd never wanted to put cubs in anyone before, but as I slid two fingers to test his slick, the act took on much more meaning. I was moving way too fast and I did not believe in fated mates. Just a legend... He was so slick, slippery, and my fingers glided inside to stretch and ready him. I forced myself to slow down and enjoy the moment.

My omega was too ready, though, and I drank every luscious drop before rising, grasping his calves and driving deep into his hot, tight hole.

No spanking, no fire, no nothing but this omega and his heat, in and out, faster and faster, waiting for him to scream out my name before pouring into him. And then out before knotting could happen.

And no marking.

Chapter Nine

Rowan

I woke with a start, flinching, but not a lot since I was in a cage of warm arms.

"It's okay. You're safe here with me," Talon whispered. His cinnamon breath wafted toward me, and what we'd done here, in his playroom, all came flooding back.

What a first date.

"I didn't mean to fall asleep. I'm—" Before I could finish my apology, Talon put his finger over my mouth.

"No more sorries, sweet omega. No more."

I sighed. "That's going to be difficult. I'm nearly a professional at apologizing."

He chuckled, tucking me in closer to his body. I craved his nearness. My wolf did as well.

Of course we did. Talon was our alpha. Our fated mate. I knew it but didn't dare say the words out loud.

Plus, there had been no knotting or marking, so there was a chance he didn't think I was his mate.

I leaned back and rolled onto my stomach. Talon ogled my form with hunger in his eyes. "What are you doing, omega? Trying to taunt me?"

"I'm going to get dressed and go home, Talon. Tonight was incredible, but I have to get some sleep for work tomorrow." I scooted toward the edge of the bed, which was easy considering the black satin sheets were made for slipping and sliding.

Talon's hand gripped my forearm and dragged me back until I crashed against his chest again. "I'm not ready to let you go. I...come home with me, Rowan. Spend the night at my home."

I gasped. This was going beyond the club and the playroom and experimenting.

And I was all in for it.

"Are you sure? I thought you just wanted me here, in this room for fun."

He growled. The reverberation shook me. "I thought so too. Convinced myself that once I had you that I might be able to let you go, but I can't. You'll come home with me?" He pressed and sealed my answer with a kiss even though I hadn't spoken it yet.

His lips were demanding and I let out a soft moan. "I have to get dressed first."

Talon smirked. "If you must."

I decided to test something. "I don't want the whole club seeing me naked."

"They will never see what's mine," he answered, low and menacing. "Not without consent."

Once we were dressed, he held my hand as we went to his office where he grabbed his phone, keys, and wallet, and to my surprise, opened one of the panels behind his desk with a press of his palm to the leather.

"I didn't know that was there," I said.

"That's kind of the point, Rowan. This leads to a private exit and to my car. Let's go."

We climbed into Talon's car, which was more like luxury on wheels. He kept his hand on my thigh for the ride, squeezing it a few times.

"Talon, this is your home?"

If an upscale, modern house had a baby with a gothic mansion, Talon lived in it. The outside was dark-gray brickwork with black accents and a huge double black front door. "It was an investment," he said, shrugging. This house was not one you shrugged at. Laid down on your face and prayed to, maybe, but not shrugged.

"It's breathtaking," I said as he came over and opened my door for me. "Don't you think?"

He raised his gaze to the house and back to me. "I've seen more beautiful things. Let's go inside. There's a chill in the air, and you are hungry."

I was, too, but didn't say anything. My hunger for him had been my priority and it was nowhere near sated.

We walked inside after he palmed the touchpad to unlock the door. With our hands linked, he pulled me into the kitchen. "Sit down. I'm going to make us something quick."

"You cook?" I asked.

"I'm a man of many talents, Rowan." He turned and winked at me.

Talon rolled up his sleeves and got to work. In only minutes, he slid an omelet onto a huge plate and added slices of toast. He pulled a container of raspberries and blueberries from the fridge. "I have water. Coffee. Milk. Orange juice. Iced tea. Sodas…" He would've gone on if I let him. I saw the vast number of beverages in his huge, double-door refrigerator.

"Water is fine. Thank you. This looks delicious." We dug in. The food was amazing but I had something to say. One of my dads used to tell me that if you have something to say and you don't, you've lied to yourself and the other person. I was no liar. "Is this...do you often bring people back here?"

He cocked his head. "Say what you mean, Rowan. You can do it. I won't bite. At least, not yet."

Talon always encouraged me. "Do you bring other omegas here? Am I...is this your usual routine? I'm just another..." I couldn't even finish the sentence.

The words were out there. No take backs.

"Rowan, you think I take omegas to my playroom and then bring them back here? That you are some notch in my belt?"

I shrugged. "I don't know. That's why I'm asking."

He stalked around the island and spread my knees to stand in between them. Cupping my face, he searched my eyes before speaking. "I haven't taken any omegas to my playroom and not because the club just opened. I only share that part of myself with those I want to and I haven't wanted to in quite some time." I opened my mouth to apologize but he spoke first. "No one comes to my home except the house staff, and I don't feed anyone. You aren't just someone in a long list of conquests, Rowan. You are special and mine."

I cast my gaze downward. His words buzzed and hummed through my mind, but it was all hard to believe.

I'd been beaten down by the words and fists of Salem for so long that even years later, I found it hard to believe anything good about myself.

"I want you to say it, Rowan."

"Say what?" I asked, meeting his stare again.

"Stand up," he commanded, but from him I didn't mind. I obeyed immediately. "Say that you are special to me. That you are mine. That I am yours. That you are beautiful and worthy and you belong to me."

I snorted. "That's a mouthful. I can't even remember all…" A slap landed on my ass, making me gasp. Gods, I liked that more than I probably should've.

"Remember what we talked about, Rowan. When I tell you to do something, it's because I care. Now, say it."

I sighed. "I am special to you. I am yours and you are mine. I am beautiful and worthy and I belong to you."

The words didn't sound as foreign as I expected.

I was rewarded with a lingering kiss which took away the sting of the spanking. Talon ran his nose up the side of my neck, inhaling deeply. "Such a good omega. So obedient and ready for me." He grazed his hand across my groin. "I'm wondering if you liked that spanking."

I nodded. "Will you only spank me when I'm naughty?"

"If you like it, we will explore the spanking some more. Have you eaten enough? Because I'm starving for you."

"I'm done eating."

Talon led me up to his bedroom where this time, the sex was slow and more fluid, if that was possible. He took his time, loving me. Whispering all kinds of words of praise and care.

"Omega, come with me," he moaned.

"Knot me." I squirmed as he loomed over me. His eyes were golden as his wolf was close, and a sheen of sweat made his body glisten.

His pumps slowed. "Are you sure? Knot you?"

I nodded. "Knot me and mark me as yours, Talon. Unless..."

"Gods, you have no fucking idea how much I needed you to say that."

Our climaxes took us with a fury. The swell of his knot grew inside me at the same time his teeth pierced my skin, right on my shoulder. I cried out in pain and ecstasy and he turned, looking at me. We were still very much connected by his knot. "Mark me, omega. Rowan. Sink your teeth into me. Show me we belong together."

My wolf rose to the surface, sharpening my canines to his, and I bit down on Talon's shoulder. He roared and his knot pulsed inside me, spilling more cum inside my body.

He was mine. And I was his. This time, it was a whole hell of a lot more than words.

He collapsed onto me. Wrapping his arms around me, he cuddled me close.

"Rest now, Rowan. Let's rest."

Chapter Ten

Talon

I brought him to my house. I never did this. Not since a certain omega shattered any illusions I might have once held. But I wanted him there, under my roof where I could see him whenever I wanted. And my wolf was pointing out very practically that we were mated. Where would he live except with us?

Many shifters actually did things that way but not me. I didn't want to drag him over my doorstep like a caveman and grunt, "My omega. You stay here all time and be pretty. And submissive."

An alpha/omega relationship and a dom/sub had some elements in common, but there were differences as well, and it was a complication not many were willing to take on long-term. Was I? Was Rowan? He lay with his head on the pillow next to mine, in the bedroom I'd imagined I'd sleep alone in forever.

And the thought of cubs rose in my mind again as well. He'd repeated what I asked him to, said he was mine, even begged me to mate him, but that could have been the moment, right? It was intense to spend time in a club like Cuffed, and if an omega had even the least curiosity about it, then it made sense that would lead to severe horniness.

But then...he hadn't asked me to try anything non-vanilla... I'd been completely satisfied, but it couldn't be the same every time. I opened Cuffed with my friends because we all were in the lifestyle. Rowan was not. Would he want to be? And if he didn't, could what was between us be enough?

His soft, even breaths were music to me. Having him curled into my side, one knee bent over my more-than-morning-wood hard cock, was torturous but also sensual in the extreme. I wanted this every morning, but not until he was ready.

"Are you awake, alpha?" His voice was rough with sleep.

"Yes, just lying here enjoying the morning."

"I stayed all night," he said. "Is that okay?"

"It was why I brought you. Did you sleep well?"

He pressed his lips to the side of my throat and kissed the skin there. "Too well. I could go right back to sleep and snuggle here with you all day."

"Best idea I've heard in years." I tousled his hair. "How did I get such a smart omega?"

"Just lucky I guess."

"Can I make one suggestion though?"

He nodded, nose brushing my earlobe.

"How about if I go downstairs and make us a big breakfast then bring it up here. We can eat in bed then take a long nap."

Rowan sat up and grinned down at me. "No wonder I picked you out of all the other doms at the club."

"You what?" I tried not to laugh, my dom side trying to decide whether it needed to take over the conversation.

"I picked you out. Who would I want but the best?"

"And we haven't even scened yet. You did want to try that, right?"

"In your playroom?"

"Deal." I pulled him down on top of me. "But if you ever feel ready to try out the main floor, it will be with nobody but me, got it?"

"Mm-hmm. What's for breakfast, Sir?"

"It's a surprise." I kissed him on the lips and rolled him to the side, giving him a quick smack on the bottom before sitting up. "You'll have to wait and see."

I was as happy naked in my own home as the next man, but for cooking, I pulled on a pair of boxers.

What we'd be eating would be as big a surprise to me as to him. Since we'd been working on the club, I'd pretty much given up eating at home, so I wasn't sure what might be in the freezer or the pantry. If I didn't manage to find anything, I'd just have to call for delivery. But my wolf really loved the idea of cooking for our omega.

Turned out, I had sausage links in the freezer and a box of add-water pancake mix as well as butter-flavored syrup in the pantry. Since I had no butter, that was a necessary element. A half hour later, I had a tray laden with food and coffee ready to take up to my omega. One thing I always had on hand was the essentials for a good cup of coffee. Dark-roasted beans, whipping cream, and raw sugar crystals.

I found him asleep again but he heard me enter and opened his eyes. "Pancakes, alpha? You're the best."

That made it harder to take him home and drop him off that afternoon. I missed him from the moment the door closed behind him, but at least I could look forward to seeing him again tonight.

Chapter Eleven

Rowan

Cuffed felt different that night. The air was charged with even more sexual energy than usual. There was a new DJ. The music had strong bass. There was something about even the music making everyone, well, I didn't really know. But the atmosphere was charged with an inexplicable energy.

Talon called me to the office as soon as I walked into the employee entrance. He kissed me stupid and said he wanted to make sure my cuff was on.

He wanted me to deliver him a drink later and promised that my tip would be fantastic.

Several times that night, I saw him come out of his office, putting out some fires. There was an altercation in one of the private rooms, and Talon intercepted the drama despite having a security team.

He even took a seat in the corner booth and watched me work. He must've had a dozen males approach him, some even being so bold as to sit next to him, only to be dismissed immediately.

Talon hadn't even looked their way.

"I take it the date went well?" Samuel sidled up to me and waggled his eyebrows.

I snorted. "I don't know if I'm supposed to say anything. Talon is our boss."

Samuel shrugged. "I won't tell. Come on. Every available omega in this place has slick dreams about Talon and meeting all his needs. Give me something."

My wolf snarled a bit inside me. "I think I'm not going to divulge. There are some things in life that should stay private and personal."

"I can respect that," Samuel said. "I can tell how it went anyway. Look at you. You're glowing. You've been smiling while drying the glasses, and no one smiles while doing that mundane work. You keep glancing to the corner booth. He's sitting there, watching your every move, Rowan. I'm telling myself that the date went well. I'm happy for you."

I nodded. "Thank you."

I took a large order for a table that the other servers seemed to be avoiding. I liked to help them when I could, if I had time. Plus, sometimes the tipsier people were, the more generous they became with their tips. Not that I'd seen many overdrinking here.

"Here you are, gentlemen." I delivered their orders but as I bent at the waist, I felt a hand on the

Such a Good Omega

back of my upper thigh. "Hands off," I said and stood back up.

"Don't you want a good tip? Or maybe you want more than just the tip?" The alpha with his crude voice and sour scent reached out and grabbed my ass. Despite his expensive suit, his words were cheap. I whirled around, ready to give him the what for when out of the corner of my eye, I saw Talon stomping over. I sucked in a breath. "Talon?"

Before I could process what was about to happen, Talon grabbed the offender by the shirt and jerked him to his feet. "Kenneth Matthews. How dare you touch one of my employees without permission." He set the man on his feet.

"I...it was just a grab, Talon. No harm." The alpha stammered out the words. Talon still fisted his shirt and reached out to tear off his ring. A red ring.

"You are banned from this club."

"What? Talon, you and I have been friends for years. Just for grabbing a cute man's ass? Are you fucking kidding me? This is a sex club. There are people doing things worse than that right there at the next table!" The man squirmed, trying to free himself from Talon's hold, but there was no use.

No one was doing anything at the next table. Members had respect for the rules unlike this man.

"Come get this fucker, William." A monster of a man with the width and girth of a linebacker came from somewhere in the shadows and grabbed the ass-grabber Kenneth by the back of the pants with as much effort as I used picking up a glass. "Turn the music down," Talon yelled, and instantly the DJ cut off all the sound.

There were lights all around the club. Talon had told me they were strategic and I knew that somehow, but in that moment, I felt like every spotlight was on me.

Talon had thrown someone out because of me.

"Listen up! We opened this club so that people of all preferences could come here and explore their desires without being assaulted and always with consent. That consent extends to every single staff member." He walked over to me and held up my arm with the cuff on. "If you see one of these cuffs on a person, you keep your fucking hands to yourself. There are plenty of ways to have your needs met without involving my employees. Spread the word. You fuck with my employees, you get banned. Now turn the fucking music back up."

Such a Good Omega

Releasing a long breath, I steeled myself to go back to work when I realized Talon had never let go.

"Talon," I breathed.

"In my office. Now."

I walked behind him and had a hard time keeping up. The man was practically sprinting. My wolf sensed that something more was going on with his mate, but we didn't know what.

As soon as the door shut, I was pushed against it and Talon's mouth covered mine. He drowned me in a searing kiss that made my knees weak. Then he pulled back and rested his forehead on my chest.

"Talon?" I asked after hearing his ragged breaths go back to normal.

"No more," he said and my chest constricted internally. What was he talking about? Did he mean me? Was I fired?

"Me?" I asked and forced my chin to stop trembling.

"What?" He raised his head. "You think I'm...you did nothing wrong out there, omega. He did. But I'm not sure I can go through that again."

Yep. This was it. He was about to fire me.

"You're firing me?" I squeaked out.

"No. I'm not. But I don't want you to work as a bartender or a server anymore. I can't take it."

I swallowed, trying to make sense of things. "Then, where do you want me to work? I have to make a living, Talon."

"I want you to come work for me, Rowan."

"I am working for you." A nervous chuckle broke loose.

"I mean for me, personally. I need a personal assistant. You're smart and capable. And I want you near. I…I wanted to hurt that man, badly for touching what is mine."

I ran my hands through his hair, knowing how it calmed him. "I am yours."

Chapter Twelve

Talon

I had a fantastic personal assistant once, but he left to mate with a wolf from a pack a thousand miles away, and it was not a job that could be done remotely. My assistant had the ability to understand what I needed and accomplish things without a lot of explanation. After his departure, I didn't have the energy to train someone else from scratch, or the time while building the club. It was easier just to do things myself.

Of course, with things up and running, I had lost my excuse. And I thought it would be nice to have my omega around all day instead of just seeing him on short breaks. Besides, my wolf was so possessive, he couldn't stand when Rowan was being ogled by the members and their guests. Nobody needed to see me lose it again.

My assistant needed to be someone I could rely on and who would keep my business private. Smart and consistent, and everything I'd seen of Rowan told me that he was the perfect person for the job.

And it meant he would be with me a lot more of the time and not out working on the floor where any one of the members might ogle or, worse, lay a hand on what...who...belonged to me. Really, most of them would recognize not only the armband but my mark, but since I spent most of my time in the office, I wasn't even out there to make sure he was okay.

I hadn't had the same office configuration or even the same office when I last had an assistant, and I was excited to help him get settled in. An inset-nook sort of area directly outside my door had been intended for my PA, but since I wasn't sure when I'd have a chance to hire and train one, I hadn't bothered to have it furnished. At this point, it housed two guest chairs, a small table between them, and a monstrous plant someone had given us.

That was over as of now. "Tomorrow morning, be here at ten. We have so much to do, you're going to be run off your feet." And right over my desk with his pants around his ankles and that rounded bottom ready for me to spank cherry red.

I hated not being able to see him tonight, but my partners and I had a meeting planned after closing to discuss how things were going in all of our departments. For most people, the early morning hours were for sleeping, but we had such different schedules, there was no way we could all connect at any other time. My responsibilities here at Cuffed involved a lot of admin duties, which began during daylight hours and bled into the evening. The others still had their day jobs in addition to what they did here, so they weren't on the property until close to opening time. I had closed out my previous office space and moved everything here so I could double down as needed.

At least I could plan for a fun day shopping tomorrow. I generally bought everything online, but why not use it as an excuse to spend time with my omega/assistant. It was not going to be easy to get anything done with him here, but we'd have to make that work. The pleasure of his company was worth any sacrifice. Even if it meant sex only at home...

The next morning, I blew all my best intentions five minutes after he arrived—fifteen minutes early—for work. He came in wearing business casual as I'd instructed when he texted me last night, and I scanned him up and down. "I've changed my mind."

"What?"

"You're overdressed. I need you to go get me a coffee and when you come back, undress outside my office and bring it in naked."

He blinked at me for only a second. "Yes, Sir." And he left.

Not a question or comment or anything. I was hard as steel.

The kitchen wasn't technically open yet, and few staff members would even be around, meaning Rowan would have to prepare the coffee himself, but the ten minutes before the rap came on the door felt like a lot longer.

And my pants got tighter by the second.

"Come in."

The door opened to reveal Rowan wearing exactly what I'd requested—nothing—a cup of coffee cradled between his hands. "Here you are, Sir. One sugar, no cream, correct?"

He'd noticed. That warmed a whole other part of me. My heart. "Yes. But put that on the desk and bend over for your spanking."

"Yes, Sir."

I pulled a tube of lube out of my top desk drawer and set it in front of his face. "Did you lock the door?"

"No..."

"Good." I stood up and went behind him, glad he couldn't see the smirk that was probably on my lips. Truly there would be nobody in the office area for at least an hour, but I wanted to see his reaction to the idea that we could be caught in the act. His flushed cheeks, uptick in breathing, and fine shiver that ran over his limbs told me the whole story.

Rowan's cheeks were pale when I laid the first smack across them, quickly replaced by pink that darkened with the repeated swats on each side. Nudity and public sex were the thing in a club like Cuffed, anywhere food was not happening, which was why it was not allowed in the tables-and-booths area. The health department had rules, after all, and even a private club like ours could be visited at any time since we charged for food and beverages. Everything sexual had to be consensual, however, and we had not done anything formal about that yet. I paused to stroke the hot skin. "We need to go over your desires and hard nos...but for right this minute, give me your safe word. It should be something you're not likely to cry out in passion. You can do green for everything is great, yellow for slow down a bit, and red for stop if you want?"

"My safe word is sanctuary."

"What?" My sex-addled brain almost had words coming in a fog, not where I should be in a dominant situation, so I mind-slapped myself into focus. "Why that?"

"Because when I walked in the door of Cuffed, I went from feeling scared and unhappy to safe and comfortable. I'd never been anywhere near a club like this, just regular bars. Some of them pretty ugh. And of course, I noticed how nice the furnishings and things were, but that wasn't it."

"No. It's a nice place to be and almost everyone had been kind and welcoming and I might want to try some of those stations one day."

"We will definitely sit down and work out the formalities, then."

He reached for the lube and handed it back to me. "Sir...would you please fuck me?"

"Since you said please." Furniture shopping might be online after all. Or tomorrow. I coated my cock and squirted a big daub between his cheeks and sank into his tight, hot hole. "It would be my pleasure."

Chapter Thirteen

Rowan

I choked down another piece of dry toast. There were very few things I could keep down for the last week or so. Probably a stomach bug since, other than the nausea and a bit of tiredness, I had felt fine.

The last thing I wanted to do was miss work.

I wanted to be with Talon all the time.

Yesterday's encounter made me eager to return the next day. To see what other ways I could please my alpha and receive, in turn, the praise I so hungered for.

Today was the first time I'd ever been late to work.

"You're late, Rowan," Talon said from his desk. I'd barely entered the room.

"I'm sorry, Talon. I haven't been...is that coffee I smell? And, oh gods, eggs?" Without a moment's hesitation, I sprinted for the bathroom next to Talon's office and vomited a whole bunch of nothing into his toilet. I heaved and heaved until my throat hurt, and my muscles around my chest were sorer than they had been for a while.

I moved to the sink after flushing the toilet, washed my face with cold water, and brushed my teeth. I'd started keeping a hygiene kit here for the late nights. When I looked up from swiping the towel over my face, Talon stood behind me, a scowl marring his perfect face.

No one that gorgeous should ever be so angry.

"I'm sorry, Talon. I really didn't mean to be late. You can take the time out of my pay. I..."

"Omega mine," he whispered and wrapped his arms around me while resting his head against my back. "How long has this been going on?"

"The throwing up?" I asked. He nodded, holding me tighter. Despite being sick to my stomach, his embrace made me feel better. "A week or so."

"What else?" he asked.

"I'm really tired lately. When I get home, I practically collapse into bed. Sometimes, I forget to eat dinner, but a lot of it makes me nauseous anyway."

He raised his head to rest his chin on my shoulder and look at me through the reflection of the mirror. "How long since our first date, Rowan?"

I gasped and whirled around and put my hands on his chest. "You don't remember?"

"I remember, Rowan. Do you?"

"Three months and two days, Talon. That night was one of the best nights of my life."

"And you've been nauseated and tired but also extra needy," he said, with a raised eyebrow.

"So? It's a bug. I'll get through it."

"Rowan," he cooed, nuzzling his nose against my neck. "Mmm, your scent has sweetened. How could I not have known?"

I shrugged.

"You've been hiding information from me, Rowan, and I'm not pleased. You were sick and tired and didn't tell me. I can't help you and support you if you won't tell me what's going on."

I shrank in place at hearing he wasn't pleased.

"I'm sorry, alpha."

"Don't do it again, or it's ten minutes on the spanking bench for you."

I barely hid my excitement. "Okay. Should I go home? I don't want to make you sick."

"Rowan, I don't think I can catch what you have. Have you considered that you're carrying our baby, sweet one?"

I felt my eyes widen. "You think that's what this is?"

Talon nodded. "I do. I want you to cancel all my afternoon meetings while I go and get you a pregnancy test. Can you do that for me?"

I nodded. "Yes."

He lifted my chin with his finger hooked underneath it. "Yes, what?" I felt the change in his tone. Sometimes the line between normal life and our other life blurred together. Especially in this case. We were speaking of something so personal.

"Yes, Sir, I can."

"Good. Go on, then. Cancel my afternoon, and I'll be back in ten minutes."

His command shifted my attitude. I was no longer focused on being sick but instead concentrating on finishing the task on time. I'd put down the phone from the last contact when Talon came in the door holding a paper bag from the pharmacy.

We went to the bathroom together and I peed on the stick. We set an alarm on Talon's watch and waited.

"Are you going to be mad at me?" I asked with a whimper.

"Mad at you?" he asked. "For being pregnant? Never, mate. Never. If you are pregnant, we made this baby together. You've done nothing wrong."

Two minutes went by as fast as eternity.

"Can you read it for me?" I asked. "Please?"

"I can." He walked into the bathroom and came back out. His eyes twinkled with something I couldn't read. "We're having a baby, my love. You are pregnant."

I gasped but paused before reacting. "Talon?"

He lifted me in his arms and peppered my face with kisses. "I'm possibly the happiest man alive right now, Rowan." But as soon as he said that, he let me down. "Aren't you, omega?"

"I am. I have my mate, and we're going to be a family. How could I not be happy?"

"It's okay if you're not. I won't be upset."

Shaking my head, I pulled him down for a kiss. "I'm so damned happy, Talon. I am. I've always wanted a baby, and having one with you feels right."

He chuckled and I was sure he felt my hardness grow between us. "I love how you are always so needy for me, Rowan. I'm glad you canceled everything because this afternoon, we are celebrating."

"Good," I replied.

He squinted. "What is it? There's something you're not telling me."

"What if I wanted that spanking now? What if I wanted to go down to the playroom here at your home. Celebrate a lot of different ways."

He growled. "I knew adding a playroom here wasn't a mistake. We have to be more careful now, but we can still play. Go downstairs and take your clothes off. When I get there, I want to see you naked and ready for me, but I will put you on the bench. Are we clear?"

I nodded as I pulsed with need. "Yes, Sir."

Chapter Fourteen

Talon

Rowan did not look well at all to me, but he shrugged off my concerns, insisting he would be fine, that omegas got pregnant all the time and lived to tell the tale. This was not like the omega I had grown to know with his cheerful attitude, and that worried me more than anything. Things came to a head late one afternoon when I suggested he go into my private club playroom and lie down for a rest, and he said things to me I hadn't even known he had the words for. To prove he was fine, he flounced out to his desk and dropped his head onto his hands, sobs shaking his shoulders.

A couple of calls led me to a healer who specialized in omega pregnancies, and I was able to get an appointment for that very afternoon. I cleared my schedule myself and then marched to the outer office and stood over him. "Omega?"

"Yes?" he said, but his head remained in his hands. "Sir? What can I do for you? Do you need coffee?"

"I need you to stand up and come with me." I waited, but he remained as he was. I opened my mouth to bark an order then closed it. Rowan responded to kindness and especially praise. "Come on, Rowan." Gently, I lifted him to his feet. "We are out of this place for the day."

He turned his face into my shirt, soaking it with his tears. "You don't really want me. Why would you?"

"Oh no, we're not going there." I guided him down the hallway and toward the employee exit. My car was parked right outside in my assigned space. "Where we are going is to the healer to make sure we're not totally screwing up this pregnancy thing."

I heard a footfall behind us and turned to see Samuel looking out the door. "Everything all right?"

"More than that." We hadn't announced our good news to anyone, but when Rowan vomited on the ground next to the car, Samuel's grin told me he got it. "No telling, okay? We want to keep things private for a bit."

"Yes, sir." He went inside and came out with a bucket of soapy water. "I'll take care of this. You two go do what you need to do, and if I can be of any help, anytime, say the word, okay?"

Rowan smiled back at him. "You've been a good friend to me since I started. Interested in godfather duties?"

"You know it."

We drove away, leaving the bar manager to clean up the mess. I didn't like asking anyone to do it, but we needed to get to the healer and find out what was going on with my grouchy, nauseous omega. I prayed to the goddess that there was nothing wrong with Rowan or the baby.

The healer was just far enough away for my anxiety to spike, but my omega was so pale and quiet, I stole a few minutes to stop at a juice/smoothie place and got him a banana/ginger/pineapple/yogurt and I wasn't sure what else because I reasoned an empty stomach is an unhappy stomach. The omega who behind the counter took one look at him and said, "Leave it to me, Daddy. I got you. This saved me with our last one. Sip it slow."

Whatever all was in it, by the time I opened the passenger side door for him at the healer's cottage-style home clinic, he looked and claimed to be a whole lot better. "I probably don't even need the appointment..."

Of course, that nonsense wasn't happening.

The healer took us in quickly and had us sit in the living room first while he asked both of us questions and made notes. Then he opened a door and waved us into an exam room that looked nicer than any I'd seen on a TV show. Shifters were generally so healthy and immune to most human diseases, so we primarily needed help with injuries too severe to heal by shifting and, of course, pregnancy support.

"Undress and up on the table, omega," the healer, Amir, said. "Your alpha said you've been out of sorts and still having some stomach upsets."

"I'm starting to feel better," he protested.

"He just lost his cookies in the club parking lot," I put in helpfully.

"And I had a smoothie."

Amir looked back and forth from one of us to the other then shook his head. "Exam time then we can talk some more."

I sat in a chair while he looked over Rowan and then he leaned on the edge of the table. "Everything looks fine, for now, and I'll give you some dietary guidance that may help settle your stomach. Try to rest when you're tired. Don't skip meals. Just generally take care of yourself. Or let your alpha help with that."

We both blushed. Great minds.

Such a Good Omega

On the way to the car, I suggested Rowan stop working, but he was having none of that.

"Fine, then move in with me, so I'm there if you need me."

He stopped and turned to face me. "Do you mean it? I'm really all right where I am."

"Where else should you live, omega? You're my mate. I love every minute of your company."

He beamed.

Such a good omega.

Chapter Fifteen

Rowan

"I'm aware of what you're offering on the property, Mr. Britt, but that particular one is worth considerably what it was when I bought it, and I won't let it go for a penny under the appraised value. In fact, I expect two offers higher than appraised by day's end, so if you really want it, you're going to have to consider what you're willing to pay." Talon owned some properties, mostly business rentals. He was smart and snapped up deals as soon as he saw them. His lack of hesitation was one of the reasons he'd gotten his hands on such lucrative investments.

I slid a piece of paper in front of Talon where he could see it. It was the specs on said property. We'd had it appraised only days before, and the numbers had come in while he was on the phone.

Talon looked up and winked at me.

No words, but I could feel the approval all the same. I'd grown more self-confident while under the care of my alpha. He praised me when I did well and, when I made a mistake, he was kind and understanding, I left those interactions without a shred of guilt or worry.

Talon was my mate. Even if I made mistakes or messed something up, his love for me wouldn't change.

I listened to him negotiate with Dennis Britt, a man who often tried to undercut my mate, but he was having none of it.

In the end, Britt paid 20 percent more than the appraisal, and Talon had turned a significant profit.

"Come here, Rowan." He patted his thigh, and I got up from my desk and sat on his lap. "You got me the numbers right on time. You were listening and I was able to close that deal because of you. You're so smart and sharp. I'm so glad I decided to bring you in to work with me."

I nearly melted into a pile of goo. "You've taught me well. Thank you, alpha."

He sat back and rubbed circles around my belly. "You're the best thing that's ever happened to me, Rowan. I should be thanking you. You're the best mate a male could ask for, and you're growing our babe inside you. What a perfect omega."

I accepted all his belly rubs and praise with gratitude.

"How about you and I go out for dinner tonight?" he asked. "What are you craving?"

I shrugged. Sometimes I felt overly spoiled. "I could eat anything."

"Tell the truth, Rowan. I can't care for you properly if I don't know what you need or want. Tell your alpha. I know you want something."

I relented. "This little wolf is craving meat. I would love to go to the Brazilian place where they bring the meat to the table."

It was hard to lay out my wants and needs sometimes, but Talon taught me how important it was. Not telling him my needs was a form of lying.

"Would you mind if I did something first?" I knew that tone. We might not make it to dinner at all.

"Depends on what it is," I teased as his hand left my belly and moved to my upper thigh.

He chuckled. "I would like to take you to the living room and give you what you need. I've been scenting your arousal for hours, mate."

"Why the living room?" I asked, curious.

"I like to experiment in all different places in the house. You know that."

"Hmm, okay. Let's go. I'm starving." He was right. I was all kinds of starving.

Such a Good Omega

We got to the living room. It was nearly dark, and he turned the fireplace on. The nights had become chilly and I was glad he decided to light it.

"Clothes off, omega. I want to see you naked on this rug."

The rug in question looked like a bearskin but was actually fake fur.

"We've never made love here," I said.

"That's exactly why it's been on my mind. I want to see you come apart right here with the fire flickering in your eyes."

Talon had specific tastes and detailed fantasies. I was happy to oblige.

I stripped and lay down on the rug. "Arms behind your head."

Whimpering, I did what I was told. "I can't touch you, alpha?"

"Not this time."

He kneeled in front of me and looked at me with such love. "I love you, Rowan James. More than anything else in this life."

"I love you, alpha. Please. Do what you will with me. I'm dying for you."

He leaned down and took my cock into his mouth. The tip of me bobbed against the back of his throat as he reached down and tugged on my sac. He pushed my knees wider. My hips rocked as he fucked me with his mouth. He knew exactly what I needed. I had been more and more needy as my pregnancy progressed and, at almost seven months, I was hornier than ever.

Talon pulled off me with a pop. "Are you slick for me, beautiful? Are you craving something more?"

"Yes, Talon. I need you inside me."

"Hmm," he said, like he was debating the decision. "Not this time, but I think we can make a compromise."

He rolled onto his stomach and leaned on one hand while the other disappeared where I couldn't see what he was doing because of my round belly. I cried out his name as he pushed three fingers inside my channel and began to pump while his mouth went back to work sucking my cock. I spread my legs wider. I wanted to reach down and twist and pinch my tender nipples, but disobeying my alpha would end with him stopping, and the last fucking thing I wanted him to do was to stop.

"Talon, I'm coming!" I cried out over and over, pouring my cum into his throat as my ass pulsed around his broad fingers.

Once I was spent, he crawled over and kissed my mouth. I could taste myself on him.

"Let's shower, and I'm taking you to eat. Then...I have another idea."

I laughed. "And you say I'm horny all the time."

"No. Not that. My wolf wants to run with yours. It might be the only chance for a while. The healer said after a while, you won't be able to anymore. My wolf is desperate to go out together."

I sat up with Talon's help. "That sounds like an amazing idea." We had tried to go out before but I'd gotten pregnant so fast, and I'd been so sick and nauseous, we hadn't done more than a "first look" shift, no run included, early on. He'd gone out without me at my insistence other times, but I just hadn't been well enough, and my wolf was content to grow the baby. At least until now...

After we got home from dinner, we waited until there was no hint of light in the sky and shifted to our wolves. My wolf's belly protruded and, while I didn't understand the magic or mystery of how, I knew my wolf was protecting our growing child inside this form.

Run with me, precious mate.

We ran for hours until I couldn't go anymore, even in my animal form. We shifted back, now fully bonded through our wolves.

"Rowan, you are everything I've ever yearned for in a mate. I hope you know that," Talon whispered as we lay in bed after another round of showers. Sleep tugged at my consciousness, but I heard his words. They shot straight into my heart.

"I've always wished for you," I answered, or tried to, and fell asleep fast.

Chapter Sixteen

Talon

For an alpha with an ownership interest in a kink club, I lived what the folks there called a very vanilla life. The fire play trunk had been put away in the private playroom because I had no desire to play with anyone else and would not be doing a demo unless and until the time came when my omega was ready to do that with me. I had hung up my fire.

If anyone had asked me a year ago if I could be satisfied with a less adventurous sex life, with only a little careful spanking to add to the picture, I'd have laughed. Even my ex, who had made me want to give up on serious relationships had been in the lifestyle.

And Rowan was definitely curious. At first, he'd said spanking was the only thing he really was interested in, but whenever he accompanied me to the club for a special event or just to visit with people for an evening, he asked me a lot of questions about what the others were up to and, when I was involved in speaking with one of my partners or a member, he sought out other omegas to learn their perspective on the varied kinks they enjoyed.

Which led to more questions for me.

Not that I minded in the least. Pregnant omega members were certainly welcome to visit the club, but they were banned from them just like amusement park roller coasters. You must be zero months pregnant to ride the St. Andrew's cross. But after the baby came, he wanted to explore the lifestyle further, with me to guide him.

I loved how we were together, everything we did, and the creativity it took to make love with his changing form. He'd lost not an iota of his drive, in fact became quite the demanding subbie. I was his daddy, his alpha, and his dominant. But mostly, I was his mate and the father of his growing baby. We lived a different life than I ever had.

The day after he moved into my house, as we sat at breakfast, I slid a folder across the table to him. "It's time."

Crunching on toast, crumbs falling onto his bump, he cocked his head. "Time for?"

"Open the folder and look." I took a sip of the decaf I always had professed to despise. But Rowan loved coffee too, and if he had to forgo the delicious caffeinated version, count me in, too.

"Preferences for omega club members?" He looked up from the screen. "I am not a member. Just your guest."

"You're a member. I took care of everything else to make it happen, but only you can do this."

"Really?" He returned his gaze to the long, multipage list. "Always okay, soft limits, hard limits...there are so many!"

"That's because it's very specific." I pointed to a list of spanking items. "See? You've been around long enough to know the meaning of hard and soft limits, right?"

He nodded. "Open palm, hand only, crop, leather flogger...wow." He riffled the pages. "How many sheets are there?"

"A lot. But we never want someone to feel like they are forced into something they aren't prepared for or didn't agree with."

He brushed crumbs off his tummy and ate another toast triangle, undoing all the good he'd done with cleaning his shirt. "Okay, so what is Florentine flogging?"

I let out a sigh. "I wish I could show you but for now, it's all about book knowledge. Two-handed flogging with very soft hide floggers. At least that's my version." I studied him, loving how his cheeks flamed. "I think you'd like it."

"And if I say being fastened into the fucking machine—is there a fucking machine?"

I shivered this time. "Yes, it's not on the main floor but in a private room that requires a reservation."

"Wow. So, say I called it a soft limit?"

"Then I could suggest trying it and, if you were up for the challenge, we would reserve the room and go slow until we could see if you like something besides my fingers and cock stretching out that hot little ass."

"When you put it that way, I'm not sure." He tapped the screen. "Gonna put it as a soft limit. At least until I see this miracle machine. Have you used it?"

"On omegas? Not lately, but they did seem to enjoy it." Which was a mild way to say they'd gotten so hot and horny, one had even passed out while spurting cum from his leather-bound cock. "If you ever give your safe word, everything stops. Instantly. And I'd take you out of the machine."

"Out of...oh my gods. How much longer am I pregnant again?"

I sat while he went over the pages, marking things and occasionally pausing to ask me a question about this or that. It took every bit of self-control I'd acquired in my life not to stand behind him and stare over his shoulder at his choices. But, when he finished, he pushed it toward me with a shy smile.

"You're okay with me looking it over right now?"

"Well, since I'm not going to be doing these things with anyone else, you're going to have to know eventually."

"True." I was reading down the first page when he tapped my hand. "Yes?"

"What if, after I get comfortable with the always ones, I want to shift some of the limits."

"Mm-hmm." Reading his answers, I was hornier than I could ever remember being.

"So, I can change my mind?"

"Anytime, omega. But you were pretty out there with your choices. I don't see you as into blood play or anything with golden showers. Not that anyone is golden showering on the main club floor."

"No. Those will never change, but some others…how are you with a whip?"

Now, I did stand up and go to him. Pulling him into my arms, I snuggled him as close as I could, given the belly situation. "Omega, whips can be deadly or incredible depending on the wielder."

"And which are you?"

"What do you think?"

Chapter Seventeen

Rowan

My work hours had changed in the last month. Our babe was growing at a rapid pace according to the healer and was large for his age. I needed more sleep, so, coming into our shared office at eight was simply not feasible for me anymore.

Talon insisted I come to the office no earlier than ten and end the day at four, no excuses.

I fought against it until Talon and I had a long talk. The next day, when I got to sleep in until nine, well, there was no more arguing to be had.

The whole thing made me feel like a pampered prince, but my mate said I was finally being treated the way I should've been all along.

More and more, I wrapped my head around those notions, but it would take time.

I walked into our new home office after a big breakfast to see something new at my desk. Talon held up a finger, and I stopped. He was on the phone and, from his eye roll, with someone he'd rather not be talking to. He didn't like long-winded phone conversations. He was a three-minutes-tops kind of guy on the phone even with me. But face-to-face? There were times when we'd stayed up all night, our only entertainment each other's conversation.

What had the alpha done now?

He hung up soon and smiled at me. "That's one of your new shirts."

"Yes. It is. One of the few that fit me now."

After breakfast, I might or might not have balanced a bowl on my belly and eaten cereal as dessert.

That was how large I'd grown.

He stood, and I gasped. I never tired of my sexy, gorgeous alpha. I chuckled.

"What's so funny?" he growled.

"My wolf is howling inside me. All you have to do is get out of a chair and I'm sent back to the first time I saw you. Dangerous and yet absolutely irresistible sitting behind that monster desk of yours. If I had been a bolder omega, I would've crawled over your desk and offered myself right then and there." I looked down, rubbing my hand over my rotund abdomen. "I couldn't very well do that now."

"You've never told me that. We might have to try that once you're all healed up from the birth."

Such a Good Omega

Tears streamed down my face. He was saying that because after the baby, I would be desirable again. I wasn't now. He was only placating me because I was carrying his child.

Talon pulled me in for a hug. "Sweetheart, what did I say?"

"It's not what you said, it's what you didn't."

He chuckled a bit but immediately cut it off. "Please tell me what I didn't say that upset you so much."

"Right now, I'm too big a cow to crawl over anything. Hell, I can barely crawl into the bed lately. Even if I could, can you imagine that sight? Not very sexy at all."

My alpha growled. "I don't like you talking badly about my mate. And, for the record, I simply thought it would be dangerous for you and the baby to be climbing on a desk. You're not going to say disparaging things about my omega again, are you?"

"I'll try not to."

"Good. Should we talk about your surprise now?"

I nodded, wanting a change of subject. He reached for a tissue on my desk and gently swiped my tears away.

"It's a kneeling chair. I know your other desk chair has been uncomfortable lately. There are a number of different sitting positions. Want to try it out?"

I'd moved to sit on the dark-gray chair when the front doorbell rang.

Soon, Vivian, our house manager, which was still weird, came up and told us there was a huge truck saying we had a furniture delivery.

Talon lit up instantly. "What is it?" I asked.

"Furniture for the nursery."

"You ordered it without me?" Gods, here came the waterworks again.

"I found a set online that I couldn't resist. If you hate it, we'll send it back. I promise."

Our office was tucked into a corner, set apart from the noise of the house. Once the men set up the furniture in the nursery, I knew my alpha had done right.

The crib and cradle, along with the dresser and changing table, were all dark oak. Made of real wood, not that thin, flimsy fake wood that most furniture was made of in the modern times.

"You bought this online?" I asked.

"I did. A few months ago. Made to order by the hands of skilled craftsman, not by a machine. You don't like them?"

In less than an hour, we had a fully furnished nursery. We'd had it painted a beautiful mint green last month. I tried to paint it myself, but Talon wasn't having any of that idea.

I walked over to the cradle, which had a gliding movement, and pushed it a bit, running my hand over the wood. "It's stunning, Talon. Really."

My alpha's chest puffed out. While I was the one in our relationship who thrived on praise, he loved it as well. Everyone deserved someone in their life who built them up. Pushed them to be their best. Fueled their confidence. Showered them with compliments that came straight from the heart.

"You did so well in choosing these. I couldn't have picked better myself. Thank you for being so generous and making our baby's nursery so special."

He came over and wrapped his arms around my waist and kissed my neck. "Omega, you make me feel ten feet tall and stronger than the strongest shifter when you say things like that."

I gasped and turned around. Grabbing Talon's hands, I put them over my belly. "Say something again. He kicks lately when he hears his papa speak."

Talon's eyes widened. "He knows me?"

I nodded. "Speak to your babe, alpha."

Talon sat on the newly delivered rocking chair and pulled me to stand in front of him. He positioned his face in front of my belly and unbuttoned my shirt so that my stomach was exposed. "Little one, you are so loved. Your daddy and I already know that you are special and smart and beautiful. We can't wait to meet you. Do you hear me, little one?"

Our babe kicked several times and the last time, simply pushed his foot toward the front of my belly and kept it there.

"I can see the imprint of his foot. Let me..." Talon frantically reached for his phone and took a couple of pictures and showed me.

Sure enough, our babe was showing off to his papa. His foot pressed against my skin so it protruded just enough to see the outline. By the last picture, it was gone.

Then Talon shocked the hell out of me. He cried. I'd never seen him shed tears before. He was always

Such a Good Omega

rock steady. Calm. Secure. Self-assured and firm in his morals and beliefs.

"Talon?" I asked.

He tugged at me, wanting me to sit in his lap. "You have given me everything, omega. I can't believe how damned lucky and blessed I am. The day you walked into that club, I knew my whole life would never be the same. Thank you for giving me this life."

Chapter Eighteen

Talon

Turned out, Amir was more advanced than just about any other healer I'd ever heard of. He had all sorts of equipment in his office like an ultrasound machine. And we had an appointment for its use. Rowan had expressed doubts, not liking the human tech much, but at his last appointment, Amir had expressed some concerns and a desire to get a look at the baby. He would have done the test right then, but the machine needed a repair or calibration or something, and we had to wait a week. He suggested we go to another healer he trusted, showing me there were others who used tech, but Rowan dug in his heels and refused.

So, here we were, with my mate's shirt pulled up to reveal his swollen belly and the healer squeezing gel over the skin. "Do you want to know the gender?" Amir asked. "Or keep it a surprise?"

We hadn't even discussed it. How funny. "What do you think, Rowan? It might make shopping easier if we know."

"True." He patted the top slope of his tummy and then grimaced and looked at his hand. "Ugh."

Amir handed him a paper towel. "Yeah, it is kind of ugh. But it does a great job, and at least we have a warmer for it now. Used to be pretty cold."

"I kind of like not knowing yet. Like we're getting to know them a bit at a time. Right now we know they kick."

We all laughed and then settled into quiet while the healer moved his device over my mate's skin.

Finally, he stopped. "Okay, you're looking good, little person whose gender shall be known before too long. They are not in a position at the moment where anything will show, if you get my drift. Look at the screen." He turned the monitor to face us, and we eagerly absorbed our first view of the baby who would be joining us in a month or so.

"They are very big, aren't they?" Rowan's voice held the appropriate concern of the man who was going to have to push that baby out of his body.

"For a baby with two wolf shifter dads, I'd say a little big, but nothing to indicate a problem. How are you feeling, Rowan?"

They discussed some recent symptoms. Sleeplessness due to an active baby, something the healer joked was only going to get worse when the baby was delivered and ready to howl. Back ache. Braxton Hicks contractions. Heartburn with certain foods, swollen feet and ankles...

At that, Amir frowned. He set down the device and turned off the ultrasound machine. "I'm going to take your blood pressure now."

He had at every appointment, so it wasn't a surprise that he planned to do that particular test, but there was an ominous tone to his voice I hadn't heard before. Steeling myself so as to not worry Rowan, I said, "Sounds good."

Amir fastened the cuff around my mate's upper arm and hit the button to inflate it. I had no idea how to read the information, so I waited to hear his report. As of our last visit, his BP had been fine, but when the healer's brow furrowed, I knew it wasn't now. Heck. "Well, looks like those swollen feet were trying to tell you something, Rowan. You're going to be having a little vacation for the next month."

"Vacation?" I asked, wondering where I could take him that was near enough to the healer for this holiday.

"That's right. When you leave here, you take your omega right home and tuck him into bed. He'll be on complete bed rest until the baby comes. I'll give you a special diet, too, and no worries or upsets for Rowan. We need to get that BP down. Do you have a cuff at home?"

"No," I told him. "But I can get one overnighted."

"I have lots of instructions for you, too, alpha daddy. If you're going to keep that baby cooking until it's due and keep your omega healthy, you've got your work cut out for you."

"I am not a lot of work," Rowan protested. "And I don't need to be in bed. I'm not that tired."

"That's not it. High BP in pregnancy can cause lots of unpleasantness. You have only one job. Stay in bed except when using the restroom or for a very quick shower, and do what your alpha tells you to do." He gave me all the orders, and I vowed to follow them to the letter. This was my family.

He argued all the way home, which I took to mean he had more fear than anything else because Rowan had never done anything but whatever was best for the baby. The healer's words had made it sound more like it was for his own good, so I had to turn it back around. "Omega, if anything were to happen to you, the baby could die too. And then what would I do? How could I survive knowing that you were both gone.

My life would be over. Please, for my sake, and the baby's, try not to get too upset, all right?"

He thrust his lower lip out. "I can work in bed."

"You can rest in bed and do as you're told. Just the way the healer said. Okay?"

"Then who will help you?"

"I will get what I need to done and use one of the guy's PAs if necessary. You have to finish growing this baby and stay well for my sanity. Okay? Deal?"

"Not sure how it's a deal if it's just do it or do it."

"It's a deal, just not a choice."

Chapter Nineteen

Rowan

"What else can we do?" I asked Amir right after he delivered the bad news and the even worse treatment plan.

"Do what I prescribed, Rowan. Please. I know this sounds like not a big deal. Some swelling. Some blood pressure issues. But trust me when I say this could be detrimental to you and your baby. This has to be taken seriously."

I sighed.

Not only had I been put on bed rest, but Talon would make me stick to the rules like a tyrant. Because he cared, of course, but tyrant.

"I understand."

Our ride home was silent. Talon's warm hand rested on my thigh, but he ground his jaw and his eyes were firm on the road. I knew my alpha. His eyes might've been trained on the drive but his thoughts weren't.

When we arrived home, we made our way to the bedroom and stood there. Saying nothing. Softly breathing.

"I can't take the silence," I whispered.

His gaze snapped to meet mine. "I'm sorry. I'm so worried. And so upset at myself. If I had taken better care of you..."

"Stop that, Talon. There isn't a layer of blame that will solve this issue. It is no one's fault, and you always take the best care of me. We will get through this. Our baby is so healthy and strong already. You heard the healer. Even if something happened today and the babe had to be delivered, it would survive and be well. It's only a month."

He frowned. "I'm supposed to be consoling you."

"Then, get over here and console me."

Talon stalked over and took off my shoes and socks. He stripped me down to my boxers and helped me into bed. Then he tucked pillows under my legs so they were higher than my heart as the healer had advised.

He sat next to me and called our house manager Vivian and told her to find a personal chef that specialized in cooking for pregnancy. I didn't know there were personal chefs who did that, but Vivian didn't miss a beat.

"We're going to get you the best food. No more sodium. Magnesium and lots of rest."

"Sounds like a thrilling time."

He didn't laugh with me. "Rowan Marwood, stop joking about this."

"Marwood? We aren't married, Talon."

He kissed my lips with great passion. "We are mated and bonded and marked. That means more than a marriage certificate or saying some vows in front of a human priest. Perhaps I haven't called you by that name before but you are Rowan Marwood."

I hadn't really thought about it before.

"I'm taking this seriously, mate. I am. I don't want anything to happen to either one of us, okay?"

Talon squeezed my hand. "I would not make it if..."

"Don't," I whispered. "Don't even entertain that thought. We will be fine."

He nodded and kissed me on the forehead, telling me he had some work to do and would be back. Despite rebelling against the idea, I gradually felt myself falling asleep.

"Rowan." The mattress sank next to me. "I have to go to the club. There are some things I need to sign and a short meeting with the other owners."

My eyes flew open and panic gripped my chest. "Without me?"

"You can't come with me and be on bed rest."

I turned my head to try and hide the tears I knew full well I couldn't. "You're going to the club without me." I wrapped my arms around my tender chest muscles.

"Mate, I don't like the accusation I hear in your voice. I am part owner at Cuffed. I have meetings to attend. I have responsibilities in order to provide for us."

"I don't mean to accuse, Talon. I...I am feeling like a spare part right now. A person of use and yet, useless. My emotions were already all over the place, and now I'm stuck here."

"You are not useless, and I never want to hear that again. You are in bed because your body is overtaxed with growing our baby inside of you. You are making another life in that body."

"There will be so many omegas there. Omegas slim and trim and ready. I..."

Such a Good Omega

Talon sat up. The atmosphere around us changed, popping and zipping with his anger and hurt. Hurt above all. "Rowan, think. Think. Am I the type of man who would go to a club and cheat on you? You think so little of me that I would betray you with another? You are my fated. My mate. My bonded. You bear my mark and hold my babe in your body. How could you?" he asked. "My love, how could you?"

With the last question, his voice cracked. I'd hurt him. I didn't even believe he would cheat on me—ever. But the jealousy and aggravation about being cemented to this bed, even though it had only been hours, drew out the worst parts of me.

I'd broken my alpha's heart.

Chapter Twenty

Talon

I was so shocked that my omega feared my being around others who he thought I might find more attractive than him. Nobody drew me like him. My wolf and I were endlessly and helplessly in love with Rowan. We followed him with our eyes when he crossed the room and felt the light leave with him when he went to the kitchen for a snack.

Most of which he was restricted from doing now.

And don't even get me started about my admiration for his growing our baby in his body. He was doing something I had no ability to accomplish and probably not nearly enough courage even if I could. This had not been an easy pregnancy, and he hadn't felt good for most of it. Yet he almost never complained.

After our exchange of words, I still had to go to work, but I stayed no longer than I had to then went out to walk around for a bit and think. My heart ached for Rowan and for me. I had not looked at another omega with anything beyond casual or friendly interest since he walked into my office the day I hired him. And I thought he understood that.

After a couple of hours, I turned back to pick up my car from the club lot. I needed to return to my omega and try to work out our differences. All couples argued, and surely it was nothing insurmountable. Fateds were still people and still subject to moods and feelings and we would just have to talk things out.

My ex had hurt me enough to make me want to never get close to another omega, yet all those feelings fell away as soon as I set eyes on Rowan. Or certainly shortly thereafter. And I'd never talked to him about the past because it seemed so irrelevant, but perhaps that was a mistake. We were to some extent the product of our pasts no matter how much we loved one another, and it was time to open up and let some of that out.

If my omega was willing.

I drove home, keeping to the speed limit with difficulty. At the last moment, I pulled into a parking spot in front of a bakery we'd been frequenting lately. Rowan loved their peanut butter cookies, so I bought a dozen and set the box on the seat next to me. Small gestures were always better than grandiose in my opinion.

The lights were on in the house when I pulled up, which meant our house manager had turned them on before leaving, presumably. Since Rowan was on bed rest, he'd hopefully not gotten up and lit them. I parked in the garage, picked up my box of treats, and headed in through the kitchen door.

"Talon?" Rowan's voice carried down the stairs. "Is that you?"

"It is. Let me just get us some tea, and I'll be right up."

"I'm so sorry, alpha. I didn't mean to accuse you or hurt you. I don't even know what's coming out of my mouth sometimes."

He sounded closer than he should have. "Are you in bed?"

A few thudding footsteps followed then a farther-away voice. "Yes, I am."

Now he is.

I wondered whether he was staying in bed as completely as I'd assumed. I stayed home as often as I could, but did have to leave sometimes. I flipped on the electric kettle and got the tea things ready, rehearsing in my mind what I might say to him when I got upstairs. I wanted to invite Rowan to share with me how he got here and also to share my own story.

But when I pushed the door open, what I saw made me lose every thought in my mind. My omega lay tangled in the sheets, his eyes bloodshot and cheeks displaying the tracks of the tears he'd shed since I left.

What a jerk I was.

"Rowan, omega mine, it will be all right." I set the tray on the dresser and rushed to the bed to enfold him in my arms. "Don't cry."

"You came back." Not the time to point out that I lived here too. "I thought I hurt your feelings and you'd never come back."

"Rowan." I tipped his chin up, looking into his beautiful eyes. "Mate, that's never going to happen. No matter what."

"But we had an argument. And I accused you of cheating on me, or at least as good as."

"Mate, we are always going to have arguments because we are people, and I didn't read what you said as that, not exactly. You were feeling less attractive, and that's on me because I need to make sure you know that you're more attractive every day." I reached between us and stroked his belly. "How could I think otherwise?"

I kissed the top of his head and rested my chin there. "But we have things to talk about. We really haven't shared enough about our pasts."

"I didn't think you wanted to hear…"

"I want to hear everything, and to share my past with you, unless you don't want me to."

"No," he said "I do."

I settled him back in bed and went to get the tray of tea and peanut butter cookies. It was going to be a long night. But a very good one.

Chapter Twenty-One

Rowan

We were in the homestretch. That's what the healer said. Only a few more weeks to go. Life in bed was boring, but Talon tried to keep me entertained with all kinds of things. Movies. Books. Games. Vivian had even come in to teach me how to knit. I'd taken to it with ease and was halfway through with a mint-green blanket for our little one.

Talon was also keeping a secret.

I called him on it, of course, and he told me, he swore, that the secret was something good. Something I would like and would make me happy and to let him have his bit of fun.

Near noon, I heard the doors open and shut several times. Vivian hadn't been up to see me, which was rare.

Something was definitely going on in this house, and I was stuck here, wondering what it was.

As though he heard my thoughts, Talon came in with a wide grin on his face. "How much do you trust me?"

I shook my head. "With my life."

"Then I'm going to help you shower and get dressed. There's something downstairs you need to see."

We showered together. Talon took over the washing since there were several parts of me that I could no longer reach without some high-level contortion.

I got dressed after a bit of a fuss about my clothes.

"Come downstairs. I promise you will love what I've got in store for you."

He scooped me up and carried me down the stairs. I was perfectly capable of walking on my own, but arguing with Talon would be pointless.

When I got to the last step and looked into the living room, there were people all in a circle and they yelled, "Surprise!"

"What is this?" I asked but smiled since this was a great break from the mundane.

"A surprise baby shower for you." Artemis ran over to hug me. A strange side hug but one nonetheless. "Come on. Let's get you off your feet."

Bronson and Jabez, the other partners, were there also. As well as Samuel and several of the other staff I'd gotten to know well at the club.

There were tables with food and gifts piled up. It was a surprise indeed.

"Thank you all for coming," I said. "This is certainly a surprise."

Arty brought the presents to me while Talon sat at my side. Some of the presents were for the baby, most of them, actually.

And some were for after the baby, for Talon and me.

I didn't expect anything less. After all, all the owners, Talon's friends, were active members of the club.

It only made sense.

"Are you hungry?" Talon asked after the gifts were done.

"Yes. But I probably can't eat the party food."

He made a grunting sound. "Actually, everything here is low salt. That personal chef went all out once I told him we were having a surprise shower for you. You've enchanted everyone in this house, mate. They all want to see you well and thriving, you and our child."

"Thank you." Talon brought me a plate and we all ate and exchanged stories.

The other owners had lots of stories. Some of them had opened clubs before. They had sold their shares for various reasons ranging from not liking the more open membership program to the neighborhood environment changing. They all brought experience and knowledge to the table.

I needed this. The laughter. The camaraderie. The stories and more than anything, the cute cake with its yellow trim and decorations, since we had decided not to find out the sex of the baby.

My mate made all of this possible.

"I think I'd better go upstairs now," I whispered to him, not wanting to alarm anyone. I could feel the stretch and pull of my skin around my ankles and shins the longer I sat.

"Rowan?" Talon looked at me with alarm.

"It's okay. But..." I raised the leg of my pants to show him the damage.

"My mate is tired. I'm going to get him upstairs, but everyone continue chatting and eating. Stay as long as you like. I'll be down soon."

Talon walked me upstairs and settled me into bed after changing into something more comfortable, his T-shirt.

Such a Good Omega

"Talon," I said as he plumped up the pillows that raised my feet. "Today was amazing. Thank you for being so caring and kind. You knew just what I needed."

When he left, I finally let out a breath. There was more going on. I'd become keenly aware of my blood pressure, and so I reached for the cuff and let the machine read me.

The numbers weren't good. Not good at all.

Chapter Twenty-Two

Talon

My mate's blood pressure was sky high and he was confined to bed for the duration... Bored out of his mind but determined to do whatever it took to carry our baby safely to the end of the pregnancy.

One thing that helped was the opening of the doors to our pasts. Once we began to speak, we'd continued to. Neither of us regarded the fact that the other had old relationships as a problem, and as I listened to his words and watched his animated features, I could not help but be thankful that we'd had our spat. It wasn't good for a relationship to have secrets.

The opening up of parts of our hearts that had been scarred closed also seemed to have an effect on Rowan's health. I didn't want to say anything yet, in case it changed, but he was less tense, and when I rubbed his feet, they weren't as swollen.

"Alpha, do you ever wonder how mates find each other? True mates," he clarified. "It's such a big world out there."

"It sure is. But I would have searched the whole world until I found you, omega. I can't imagine living without you." I set his right foot down and reached for the other. Smoothing the arch, I felt the pulse there and marveled at the life force in my hands. "I believe, now, that Fate will make sure we have a chance to meet our fated. Maybe some choose not to accept the gift."

"But how sad is that?" He tugged his foot back and sat up on the bed. "It doesn't scare you?"

"No. Not when you're right here. Give Fate some credit. Look what they did for us." I continued my massage, putting his leg in my lap and kneading my way into his calf. My omega carried a lot of tension in that part of his legs, and there was so much there now.

"I know you love me and you are my fated, but I feel like such a sack of potatoes, lying here in bed and doing nothing while you work and support us and everything."

"I am glad to help because I can. And we have the house staff to help. Omega, the reason you are in bed is to help your blood pressure. How is that doing?"

He looked past me.

"You have been taking it?" And why hadn't I?

"Yes, but probably not often enough."

"Can I take it now?" Releasing his leg, I got up from the bed and opened the nightstand drawer to withdraw the cuff we kept there. "Is this all right?"

"Okay." He held out his arm and I fastened the cuff in place. "But it's probably awful."

"Relax if you can, and let's see." He should be having peace and quiet and here I was making it all worse. But I needed to know whether he was doing all right. If not, I'd call Amir right away. I watched it inflate and ease back while I studied the little digital screen. "Omega, look."

Chapter Twenty-Three

Rowan

Three words I never thought I'd hear myself say: Pregnancy Yoga Lessons.

But here I was, stretching and moving along with the instructor Talon insisted be brought into the house, even after I showed him the plethora of videos available for free online.

That man didn't listen.

My blood pressure had corrected itself, which Amir said was a rare thing but sometimes happened with shifters, and with my due date coming up, he signed off on the yoga provided my BP continued to be normal. I had to test it before and after each session.

After my session with Jada, she insisted on a small meditation. I turned around to roll my eyes but complied, opting for my chair next to the bed instead of trying to get down onto the floor only to need help getting back up.

I'd made that mistake day before yesterday when she insisted on the same thing.

I closed my eyes and listened intently to her words. Words of calm and reassurance. Sometimes her counsel during these meditations was so on point, I would swear Talon had given her a Rowan point by point email, telling her what to say.

"Breathe in calm and breathe out turmoil and anxiety. All is well."

I repeated the mantra. I wouldn't easily admit it to anyone except Talon, but as much as I fussed and kicked up dirt about the meditation, I thought it was helping.

I had made it to week thirty-eight and so, I was all clear. Whenever this babe of mine wanted to come, we were ready.

All of us.

Once the session was over, I stood to thank Jada. When I did, a great whoosh that started in my lower belly released a gush of water that traveled down my legs.

"It's okay, Rowan," Jada said. She immediately got on the phone and called Talon. Talon bounded up the steps and was in front of me in seconds.

"I called the healer. He's on his way. Would you like to shower first?"

Such a Good Omega

I tipped my chin in Jada's direction. Didn't really have it in me to speak yet.

"Jada. I'm sorry. Thank you for the session. Your pay is already in your account." He dismissed her the way he dismissed me after my interview with him. When my alpha dismissed someone, they left. Promptly.

It was his way.

"Yes, I need to shower," I said.

Talon washed me and, while we were drying off, an aching pain clamped down on my lower back in a wave, making me cry out and brace myself on the edge of the counter.

"Talon, I think this baby is coming right now."

"The healer is on the way."

I laughed. It sounded hysterical. "The baby doesn't give two shits, Talon. They are coming. Now."

We had planned on a home birth but not like this. There was a sterile tub and water to be drawn, but we had no time for that. My mate thought fast and ran some slightly warm water into our huge tub.

"Get in," he said as the water still ran.

"I think...I think I need to push." I grabbed hold of the edges of the tub and bore down, pushing all my force down into my hips and the channel where the babe would emerge.

"You're pushing already?" Talon was on his knees beside me. He had never looked so helpless before. So powerless.

If my alpha hadn't built me up in the months since he'd loved me and known me, I might not be able to be the strength our babe needed.

But he had.

And I had it in me to deliver this baby.

"It's..." I cried out. "I think that's the head. Gods, I'm on fire!"

I raised up in the tub to give the push of a lifetime, more than ready to get this baby out of me.

The healer appeared in the doorway and rushed to my side. He nearly jumped into the tub, trying to check out what was happening. "Your baby is crowned. Two or three more pushes and we're there."

"Okay. I've got this. I'm strong and capable." I thought I said those words to myself, but, when Talon leaned over and kissed my temple, I knew he had heard.

"Yes, you are. You so are."

With those sentences, I pushed with all my might. The first one released the head of our babe, and one more drove him out of me with a great whoosh of pressure.

"It's a boy," Amir said. "Ten toes and ten fingers and looks like a big, healthy boy at that. Good job, Daddy."

He placed our son on my chest. The babe immediately quieted and nuzzled against me.

"Look what we did," I said to Talon who had rivers of tears rolling down his face. One of his hands was on the back of my head and the other stroked the back of our child.

"What's his name?" Talon asked.

"Lincoln James Marwood," I said. "We can call him Link."

"Hello, Link," my mate cooed at our boy. "I'm your papa and this is your sweet, strong, daddy. We love you so much."

Amir took Link so he could be cleaned up and weighed and measured. Vivian came in and after delivering the afterbirth, helped me from the tub. I could see how torn Talon was, looking from me to the babe and back again. I insisted he stay with Link.

Finally, a few hours later, after we were both checked over, Amir left and asked us to call if there was anything we needed. He made sure Link was latching well and drinking, which he was, like a champ. Vivian brought in some snacks and told us to call when we wanted a real meal.

All was quiet. Amir said my blood pressure and the swelling would go down and I would heal faster than a human, of course, but to take it slow.

"He's perfect." I handed Link to his papa. Talon sat next to me and hadn't moved from that spot.

"He is and so are you. I can't get over how strong you've become."

I nodded. "You made me strong."

"No." My mate shook his head. "You were strong all along; you only needed the proper praise." He lifted his gaze to me and kissed my lips, lingering longer than a peck. "I love you, Rowan. I'm grateful every day for the moment you walked into that interview."

"I love you too, Talon. You're the best mate I could've ever asked for."

Epilogue

Talon

The list of acts Rowan wanted to try, was hesitant to try, and definitely hadn't wanted to try laid on the table between us. "I know it's too soon for any of this, but as soon as Amir signs off, I want to start trying some of them."

His determined tone was music to my ears, but I needed to be sure. "You aren't saying this because you think I need more than we already have between us? I can't imagine being any happier than we are."

"It's for me. I've been thinking about it since I first walked into Cuffed, and with the pregnancy, we had to put that on hold, but now is the time, I think. Well, not quite now, but you get it."

"Yes, I think I do."

"Plus, I hear there's a real call for you to do that fire demo."

I was incredibly happy with my little family, but if there was room in our life for club life, I wasn't going to say no. Sure, Cuffed made money, but that wasn't why my partners and I opened it. At least not entirely.

We'd had a vision for the place, somewhere we could practice our kinks as well as offer a safe and welcoming place for others to do the same. And I could already see my omega lying on the table while I prepared the tools and safety equipment. The spotlight on his perfect skin, the flame flicking to light...

A cry pierced the fantasy, our son demanding our attention. We looked at each other and laughed. Our time for club life would come, but at this point, we weren't even leaving Link with a babysitter. Still, it was something to look forward to.

"Coming, Link." I stood up and waved Rowan back into his chair. "I'll change him and bring him to you for his dinner." My mate and I were a team in all things. He was also half owner of my share of Cuffed now, although that was a surprise I planned to spring on him whenever he made his first visit. Whenever that was.

I picked up our son and cuddled him before carrying him over to the changing table. "You have the best daddy, Link."

He wriggled as I held him with one hand and reached for a fresh diaper with the other. And together we had the best son. A loving, happy life.

An Excerpt From Strong Alpha

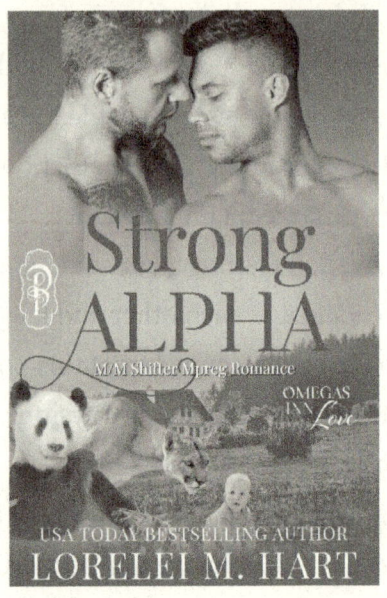

I'm too busy for an omega. That's what everyone tells me. My passion is my work and my work is my passion. When those two things collide, there is no such thing as a day off.

I'm a strongman, and that means my days are structured from the time I wake up until the time I collapse into bed, when I'm prepping for a competition. My meals. My workouts. Even my free time, all of it is consumed by my work. But my mountain lion craves an omega to care for. Someone to be by my side. A loving fave to seek out in the crowd. If

I had my mate, my life would be whole. No scheduled time for dating for this alpha. So, when I receive a letter from Franklin at the Bearclaw Inn, I take things into my own hands and get on the plane.

They say that a match is guaranteed if you go, and I'm not wasting a second of this weekend.

Strong Alpha is the sixth book in the Omegas Inn Love Series. It is a sweet with knotty heat MM shifter mpreg romance featuring a competitive athlete and gym owner alpha mountain lion, an omega panda with zero interest in exercise, the magic of Franklin and his Bearclaw Inn, and a guaranteed HEA. Each book in this series can be read as a standalone. If you like your alphas hawt, your omegas strong, and your mpreg with heart, download your copy today.

Chapter One

Shane

"I think I found the one," an alpha on the hack squat machine told his coach. If he was able to talk in depth about an omega, then he probably wasn't lifting enough. Lifting wasn't like running. If you could carry on a conversation, then you were doing something wrong.

Besides, while I was happy enough for my friends and clients finding their mates, it only stabbed me with the reminder that I hadn't found mine. And with the way I trained and worked, I might never find him.

I completed my finisher set and wiped the rivers of sweat from my brow. I let out a long breath, listening to my heart recover as more trails of salty sweat poured down my back.

Why did I do this again? Oh yeah. Because I fucking loved it. I loved the cause and effect of it all. If I put in the work, I saw results. Period. My niche was being a strongman, meaning being as strong as possible in every event in the contest both globally and nationally.

The thing was, it took up all my time. Every ounce of it.

I showered in my private shower, the full bathroom next to my office. In addition to my contests, I had sponsors and all kinds of social media platforms. Lines of protein shakes and supplements and apparel. So many side hustles, I had a team to run them for me.

Sometimes, it was hard to breathe.

"Good workout?" My cousin and part-time trainer and social media manager strolled into my office and took a seat while I read emails, or pretended to. I spent a good amount of time daydreaming lately, even in the middle of sets. I should've been concentrating on my form, on setting new personal records, but instead, the other side of me, the mountain lion side, was demanding I go out and find a mate.

"Very." I shrugged off the half-truth.

"You're not eating," he said, glancing up at the calendar on the wall. It took up almost the entire space and, while it stayed mostly the same, there were some variants to keep things fresh. Fresh as in, I would have my meals at different times and maybe a meeting with a new sponsor—try out a new protein shake flavor.

But basically every day was eat, sleep, workout, work on my business. Rinse and repeat.

Such a Good Omega

While building up my body and being strong had been a priority since high school, I had to admit that things had changed inside me.

Yes, I still wanted to be the strongest man in the world, but I also wanted more. I wanted an omega. To have a family. Children. A fucking hour to myself.

Sure, I had days off but they were few and far between. They were spent alone, watching TV, eating my meal-prepped food.

Some would look at my life and see a dream. And they were right. The way I lived was a dream.

But, curse me, I craved more.

"Right. I got a little off track." I almost stood from my office chair, but Chad pulled one of my meal-prep containers from his lap. Hadn't even noticed he had it.

"One step ahead of you." He passed me the container. Bison burgers, green beans, and sweet potato, one of my favorite combos.

"Thanks."

Chad nodded, but there was more he wanted to say. I popped the lid on the container and began to eat. "Is there something you need to talk about, Shane?" he asked.

"Why?" I asked another question avoiding his. He had an omega. Three sweet little girls as well. He went home at night to a warm bed and people who loved him.

I went home to...me.

He shrugged. "You seem like you're in another world lately."

I sighed. "Just some things on my mind."

He nodded. "I'm here if you ever want to talk, you know. Not just about the workouts or the business. When's the last time you went out, Shane? I can see if we can schedule you some free time."

"Look at the schedule for next weekend," I said, knowing that I'd demanded the time off. Didn't know what I was going to do or how I would spend the time, but I needed a break from the walls of the gym, the weight on my shoulders. All the weight on my body both physically and mentally had begun to strangle me while simultaneously building me up.

Chad rose from his seat and grabbed his tablet from his office, coming back in with a whistle on his lips. "Didn't know the strongest man in the world got a day off, much less a weekend," he chuckled.

"I need it."

After a few meetings, I went home and collapsed on the couch with a recommended book on self-discipline from one of my friends and a meal of

Such a Good Omega

chicken breast and broccoli. I stuck to their meal plans most of the time but lately found myself sneaking a bit of ice cream at night.

A little pleasure for myself.

Before I started in on the reading, I took a look at my personal mail. There was a blue envelope I didn't recognize. As I turned it, I saw it was from a Franklin from a place called the Bearclaw Inn.

I'd never stayed at a place called the Bearclaw, and I knew no one named Franklin.

The letter inside surprised me even more.

A weekend at his inn, free of charge, and on the exact dates I'd taken off.

Tingles slid down my spine at the coincidence.

What in the hell was the Bearclaw Inn?

Chapter Two

Zhang

Weekends are the best.

While aware that many people thought so, pandas had a reputation for enjoying our leisure time, and I was the poster boy for that. My entire life focused around those precious two days where I had few commitments and could engage in my hobbies of sitting around the house, sitting by the nearby lake, lying on a floatie on the lake, and my very favorite, the backyard hammock. I picked this house specifically because it had two perfect trees for hanging the hammock.

Not that pandas were lazy...not completely. When at the office, I did my fair share and completed all tasks assigned to me. My supervisors never had to micromanage me, nor would I have tolerated it if they did. The last one left a couple of months ago and had not been replaced. The best way to maintain my serene and happy life was to avoid annoyance, and this situation was perfect.

Such a Good Omega

I also avoided exercise. Perish the thought. Our company health plan included a health club membership. Which I loved because it had a sauna and hot tub, even if I did have to walk past a lot of machines, I had no interest in touching to get to them. But, to each their own, and I did not mind watching those who made use of them. If they were happy, I was happy to appreciate their muscle tone.

Unfortunately, they were not interested in someone who would not sit down on one of those seat thingies and lift up heavy weights alongside them. Or so it seemed anyway. It was like I didn't exist.

My job in the insurance industry paid well enough for me to own my home and enjoy my time off, but I'd never get rich doing it. Not that I cared. As long as I could replace the hammock from time to time, all was good.

This afternoon, I was on my way to the gym, feeling the need to unwind after a particularly rough day at work. In general, it only occupied half my mind at best, but we'd had a meeting where we were informed that one of the supervisors was leaving, and they wanted to congratulate the person who was being promoted to replace him.

Sitting at the big oval table in the conference room, I looked around at the others from my department. As the employee who'd been there the longest, I had seen a lot of supervisors come and go, but it rarely made a difference in my well-ordered life. The best thing about my job was that I didn't have to take it home with me. At the end of each day, I climbed into my car and left, shutting off the "work" portion of my brain until the next time I sat down in my desk chair.

Everyone stood up to help themselves to the catered food set out on the sideboard. Lots of panda shifters were vegetarian or close to it, but I had never wanted to restrict my diet that much. Sure, on my own, I might eat salads or fruits and veggies most often. Along with desserts. But if the powers that be wanted to put out trays of hoagies, sign me up.

I waited patiently in line then filled my plate with an Italian Delight sandwich, scoops of potato salad and cole slaw, and eyed the multitude of brownies. *I'll be back,* I promised them while passing the huge platter set at the end of the table. Usually we didn't get anything this good for a meeting. Whoever they were promoting must either be one of those who kissed up to management or someone who would need encouragement to accept the position. A bunch of stuffed and happy coworkers clapping when your name was announced made it really hard to say no. Or so my friend Angelica told me when they put her in charge of accounts receivable, probably the worst position in the worst department in the company.

Yeah, whoever they had in mind was going to have to accept or look like a real jerk. Also, once someone turned something down, they were basically regarded as not a company person and might as well be on their way out.

I sat down with my plate and can of fizzy water, ready to enjoy my lunch. Most people wanted promotions, didn't they? My lack of ambition was nothing to be proud of. But I loved my life. The only thing that would make it better was a mate, but none of those gym rats would give me a second glance. Not that I wanted them to. Much.

"If everyone has their lunch, it's time to get the meeting going." The manager over our department and two others were running the show because we were here to replace the supervisor who would have normally handled things. Technically, according to federal and state regulations, we should have gotten time to eat before they began. A meeting was not a qualified lunch break. Someone who used to work here took that matter to HR once. Did I mention they no longer worked here?

A rustle of sandwich wrappings being set aside showed how much nobody wanted to attract attention. I'd already unwrapped mine, knowing how this worked.

"As the email inviting you to this little party mentioned, we are here to celebrate a promotion. It's someone who has worked long and hard here and deserves the step up." A party or celebration did count as a break...looked like HR had reacted.

We all looked at each other. Who would it be? Did the person already know, or was it a surprise? I didn't see any expressions that indicated someone being celebrated. A prickling at the base of my spine began when Glen Collins, the manager, walked around the table. In my direction.

He arrived at my side and held out his hand. "Everyone, a round of applause for Zhang, your new supervisor." He shook my hand and pulled me to my feet, ushering me to the head of the table. Without my plate. That probably shouldn't have been in my mind. Panda thoughts.

Such a Good Omega

No thank you. I am not worthy of this honor. I can't possibly...

I got a standing ovation.

Changing my speech plans. "Thank you, Mr. Collins. I don't know what to say."

"It's Glen for supervisors, Zhang. Just say you'll continue to be the excellent employee you always have been in this new role."

"You know I always put the company first." Whose words were these? "And my door will always be open to anyone who needs my help." Not that the supervisor had a real door. It was an office off the main shared space with an archway sort of thing.

About the Authors

Lorelei M. Hart is the cowriting team of USA Today Bestselling Authors Kate Richards and Ever Coming. Friends for years, the pair decided to come together and write one of their favorite guilty pleasures: Mpreg. There is something that just does it for them about smexy men who love each other enough to start a family together in a world where they can do it the old-fashioned way.

Sign up for our Newsletter here.
Check out the Shifters of Distance
Lorelei's Amazon Page

Made in the USA
Middletown, DE
21 February 2025